THE BELGIAN BEAST

JANAE KEYES

Edited by
DELIARIA NICOLE DAVIS

To the country I've grown to love since 2011.

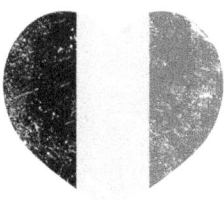

Vive la Belgique, Je t'aime.

CHAPTER ONE

MARC

The roar of the crowd filled each and every crevice of my body.

The exhilaration pumped through my veins, my name on the lips of every single person in the room. The on-going chants surrounding the octagon stimulated the resounding thud of my heart through my ears.

"*Bel-gian Beast! Bel-gian Beast!*" They droned as a collective unit, egging me on, preparing me for what was to come.

Nowhere—no one—had kept me as grounded as the cage had. This was home. I'd been told the love and sweetness of a good woman was the only high which could top this, but in my experience, there was no such thing as a woman who could stop my heart with a single glance.

Only the octagon could give me pause and it would always be that way.

The cheers grew louder until an eerie, haunting silence filled me, and pulled me away from the present.

"And you think you're a man? A scared bitch. Yeah, that's you, just a scared little bitch like your mother."

I was thrown violently back into the origins of my story. It was the voice of my dead father, drunk as fuck like always, echoing through my head. He always seemed to be there when I fought. The ferocity of those moments of my past was what brought me to my present, and I could never ignore it. It was my fuel. He pushed me to the edge, I could never go back.

His slurred as shit words were always in my head. His boastfulness pulsed through his words spoken in perfect Flemish Dutch. My father was proud of his Flemish origins and made sure everyone knew it. Hell, he had 'Vlaanderen' tattooed on his arm with the lion right under it proudly representing his region.

When I finally stood up to him, he'd insulted my masculinity as if that was a worry of mine.

"Come on. Hit me. Do you really think you can hurt me, little punk?"

"Stop! Please! Don't hurt Marc. I'm begging you." The voice of my angelic mother cut through his insults, begging him to stop, but she was too late. Years of watching him abuse her and suffering abuse at his hands had led to that infinitely defining moment.

"Did you hear that, Marc? Your slut mom is trying to save your little ass. Come on, Marc, be a fucking man and hit me!"

The bell rang through my senses and the chants of

my surroundings returned. The scent of blood and sweat filled my nostrils. That smell was my comfort.

The cheers and whistles, along with the resounding of my infamous nickname, *the Belgian Beast*, permeated the room as I held my position against my opponent in the cage, and I hit him the same way my father had demanded I hit him. My fist slamming into his face and blood sputtering from his mouth, spraying across my pale arms, leaving them peppered in crimson red.

The room fell into utter chaos and excitement at each punch I laid into the guy who dared fight me. This guy wasn't like me, he hadn't had to kick his dad's ass at the age of fifteen. This guy didn't have to take up fighting to make a living before he was old enough to drive a fucking car. This guy *wasn't* the Belgian Beast, but *I* sure as fuck was.

I would give it to him, he had some fight in him and with each jab and kick I laid into him, he'd stumble but came back at me eager to show the world someone could tame the beast.

That wasn't the case. Nobody could tame the beast. In only a moment, he was down. I was on top of him, my fists laying fury to his face until I saw his eyes rolled back in his head and bright red blood ooze from his mouth.

As the ref called the fight, I rose, victorious as help was ushered in for the unconscious guy on the ground. I'd done my job and that's what mattered to me. I put up the good fight through skills I'd learned since I was a kid.

I remained undefeated.

"And the winner is, the Belgian Beast!" The announcer echoed through the auditorium and the crowd went insane, chanting as the ref lifted my arm into the air to claim my victory.

Another fight down.

At this point, after years of fighting, they all seemed to blend, except for the few standouts. This was another day at the office. I made my living by the fight and would do it until I couldn't anymore. It was what I knew. It gave me what I needed. It was my way of working through the frustrations of my life and providing for those I cared about.

Leaving the octagon behind, I was patted on the back by my trainer and manager, Jean. The short yet feisty gray-haired man took me under his wing when I was only a kid and he made me into the beast I was. He harnessed the fight I had in me and taught me how to use it.

"Excellent!" He cheered proudly as he continued to slap my bare, sweaty back proudly.

"Get my pay," I grunted in demand as I left the chaos of the arena and found the solace of the locker room.

After a fight, I was left on a adrenaline rush that raced through my veins and kept my heart pounding in my chest. Entering the locker room, I let out a loud roar which echoed off the beaten up metal lockers and reverberated throughout the room.

There were guys getting patched up and showering

after their own fights. They all paused at my loud entrance. A simple nod of congratulations was given by another fighter and I nodded back. I wasn't one for small talk. I came and did what I had to do. I didn't fuck around. I'd made a few connections in my world, but I hadn't sought them, they found me.

It wasn't until I was older I found myself appreciating my father for being a piece of shit. By this time, he was already dead after crashing his car while drunk on the Brussels Ring. I was glad as fuck he was dead. Nobody needed him around. The man beat the shit out of my mother every night with myself and my sister watching. He'd beat us too sometimes when he was drunk enough. The worst nights were when he'd gambled everything away. Our stomachs were empty and then he'd lay into us over his shortcomings. Shit bastard.

"Marc, ton argent," Jean announced in French, as he pulled me out of my fog. He handed over a thick envelope.

I sized it up and peeked inside. Ten-thousand Euros in cash. I knew exactly how much it was simply based on the weight in my hands.

"You fought good. Not your best but he wasn't up for your full force anyway."

I shrugged.

Jean shook his head at my usual reaction.

After a fight, I found myself living in a fog of memories. Dad's voice practically pulled them to the forefront of my mind. They were things I'd rather forget.

Standing abruptly, I had to fight through the fog and into the clarity I'd won another fight and was covered in sweat and blood splatter. With a grunt, I shoved myself past him and the other fighters standing around until I reached the showers.

The stink of men filled the thick, steamy air as I strolled to a shower-head and twisted the metal knob to turn the water on. Steaming hot spray immediately came forth and I immersed my body in it. I washed it all away, from the words of my demented father to the blood of my opponent. All of it washed down the drain as the scorching water trickled over my bald head and heated body.

When I finished my shower, I stepped into the locker room with a towel around my waist. There were fewer guys standing around now as the fights had finished for the night. For now, it was only me, a few stragglers, and Jean who waited on the bench near my belongings as he usually did.

Jean was a good guy. One of the few good guys around and I considered him more than my coach and manager, he was a father-figure. I was barely fifteen when I met him, my eyes peering into a Mixed Martial Arts gym in awe of what the guys were doing. Jean was the owner of the gym and saw this scrawny kid standing outside. He invited me in, and my training began.

"Ça va?" He asked with genuine concern. The man

knew the demons which haunted me, but never pushed me to reveal them. It was all in my own time.

"Ça va," I answered as I wasn't in the mood to talk. I wasn't much of a talker anyway. I kept my issues and emotions inside. I allowed them to battle in my mind and in my heart without spilling them out unless I really needed to. Jean understood this and let me be.

As Jean left a slap on my back, I glanced up at the man who gave me a proud beaming grin. Slowly a smile crept onto my lips as well. I knew I did good and it was nice to have that one person who believed in me from the first moment. The man pushed me hard and I intended to continue to make him proud.

"What are your plans for the night?" Jean asked as I pulled my shirt over my head.

"Going to see my sister and her kids. Taking them some food," I told him while I finished dressing.

"How is Sophie?" He asked as I reached my hand into my envelope and pulled out a couple of thousand euros and handed it over to him as I did after every fight.

I shrugged at his answer.

Sophie was all over the place and I never really knew how she was doing from one day to the next.

"Tell her I say, hello."

"I will." Standing tall, I threw my bag over my shoulder and gave him his own slap on the back. "See you," I muttered to my old friend as I picked up my silver and black motorcycle helmet from the bench.

"Bonsoir. We'll talk about your next fight at the gym," he noted.

I nodded simply and walked out of the locker room.

Once out in the cool air, I was hit with screams and cheers from those who waited at the back door in hopes of getting a photo with me or an autograph. I grunted in frustration. I didn't do autographs after fights. After a fight I was still riding this rage filled high and couldn't dare socialize with fans. I'd rather do it at another time. It wasn't that I wasn't approachable, because I could be, but after a fight it was a no go.

All in all, I didn't fight for the fame and the glory, I fought because it kept my family afloat and allowed me an outlet for my rage. Fans came with the territory. I loved that people enjoyed me and what I'd worked hard for.

Ignoring the flashes of camera phones and my nickname being shouted. I continued onward toward the street where my motorcycle was parked and waiting for me. I secured my bag in one of the saddle compartments and placed my helmet on my head. My helmet did help muffle out the noise and calmed the intensifying anxiety I fought with daily.

Once on my bike and in gear, I zipped down the street away from the crowd and into my element. The streets of Brussels blurred past as I drove toward my first destination with the wind whipping past me and my quickening heartbeat slowing. The tenseness in my jaw released and calm began to wash over me, but I knew my calm wouldn't last long. It was a yo-yo of intense senses that kept me entrapped.

It wasn't long before I found myself in one of those neighborhoods most tended to avoid, especially in more recent years. Molenbeek didn't have the best reputation of all the cities that made up the capital region. The mostly Moroccan populated neighborhood had a flavor right out of the streets of Morocco itself. I quite liked it in a way, but the rampant crime made me fear for my little sister who called the place home.

I pulled up to an open Delhaize. Luckily, I had a few minutes before the store was supposed to close. Parking my bike, I secured it to a pole, eyeing the men who stood around loitering and smoking cigarettes in the shadows. Lucky for me, I could easily kick their asses and I'm sure my tall, muscular body made me the least desirable victim.

"Bonsoir," my voice was deep and commanding as I passed them and trotted into the automatic doors of the store. I could barely hear their muttered greetings as the door closed behind me.

Taking a small hand basket, I made my way quickly through the store. I grabbed the essentials with a few other items, including a few chocolate bars. I paid and went outside. One of the men gave me a nod as I passed them once more. I didn't return to my bike, but instead began up the street with the bag of groceries in hand.

The late summer night wasn't warm, but also wasn't as cold as most nights usually were in

Belgium. Savoring the last few nights of summer, the neighborhood was filled with life even at the late hour. Kids were out riding bikes and drawing on the sidewalks, while adults stood around chatting and having a beer.

My sister's building had a few of her neighbors on the front porch. They all greeted me warmly as they did when I arrived for a visit. As usual, when I stepped inside, there was a notice the elevator was down, so I took the stairs.

The stairwell was dimly lit, and the lights flickered as I scaled the stone stairs up to the heavy fire door of the third floor. Pushing the door open, I stepped into a narrow hallway. In the hall I could hear televisions blaring, ethnic music playing, couples fighting, and children playing. I walked toward the sounds of children playing through the last door in the hall, apartment 4C.

I knocked hard with the hope of breaking over the loud screaming of the children and moments later was rewarded with the door swinging open. A thin tanned man stood in the doorway.

"Shalom, brother," I greeted the guy who'd been my sister's on and off boyfriend for years. Basir was Moroccan and had begun dating my sister when they were in secondary school. Their turbulent relationship had lasted nearly ten years and spawned two children.

"Marc, mon frère, ça va?" He allowed me into the tiny apartment my sister'd managed to get, but I usually paid the rent for.

"Ça va, et toi?" I asked over the loud children who continued to play and enjoy one another.

"Okay," he answered dimly as he rubbed his hand over the back of his head and sighed. It was easy to notice someone was missing from this picture, my sister, Sophie.

"Sophie has gone again, hasn't she?" I already knew the answer. "How long?"

"A few days now," he told me as we stepped into the living room and the kids peered up from their game to see who'd entered their home. I saw the eagerness in hopes it was their mother. There was disappointment, but they gave me excited grins as they bounded in my direction.

The oldest at three, Najah, leapt into my arms and snuggled against my chest. The little dark-haired girl was almost the spitting image of my sister with a slight ethnic flare from having a North African father. The little boy who trailed behind her was only a year and a half and looked more like his father, except he had bounding blond curls on top of his head.

"Oncle Marc," Najah cheered happily.

"Onc Marc-Marc," the little one, Kamil, attempted to copy.

I bent and pulled him into my arms in a tight hug as well.

Sophie and I were both damaged from our childhood but went about healing in different ways. I poured my anger, rage, and post-traumatic stress into the octagon. Sophie, on the other hand, took after our father. She began drinking young and it didn't take long for her to pick up the gambling. On occasion, she would disappear for days at a time when she fell down the rabbit hole. Luckily Basir was a good dad and did what he could to keep consistent in the kid's lives. Our mother and I also did our parts.

"I brought you something," I reached into the grocery bag and produced the candy bars I'd gotten from the store.

"Oh, merci," Najah cheered as she grabbed her Kinder bar from my hands and began to tear open the wrapping to get to the goodness inside.

Always following the lead of his big sister, Kamil took the other bar but struggled to open it. "Ci, ci."

Beaming at the little boy, I helped open his bar before he tore into the chocolate. I allowed the kids off my lap and they both took their chocolates with them and sat in front of the television. I turned back to Basir who gave me a weak smile.

The man was only in his early twenties already sprouting gray hairs and had bags under his eyes. He worked two full-time jobs and a few other part-time and odd jobs to do what he could for my sister and his children.

"I'll have to take the children to your mother. I've missed work," Basir explained and I completely understood. He had to do what was best even in my sister's absence.

"I brought a few things for the house," I handed over the grocery bag to my brother-in-law who gave me a weak smile of thanks. I'd always make sure they were taken care of and had a roof over their heads. It wasn't completely my sister's fault. I grew up in that shithole too. I only hoped she could fight her demons hard enough to get past where she was.

AFTER BIDING my sister's boyfriend and children goodbye, I returned to Delhaize where I'd left my motorbike. Even though I'd chained it purposely to a pole, it was gone. The store had closed and there was nobody around.

"Fuck," I grunted angrily as I balled my fists. Luckily, nothing I'd left with my bag was of much importance. My gym bag only held my soiled clothes and nothing more. I'd had a bike stolen before.

Deciding to let the matter go, I shrugged. I could always buy another one. It was a mild inconvenience. In the past, I would have raged over the matter, but it was only a blip. I had to let my anger out elsewhere. Tomorrow, my fists and a bag would settle my rage.

Taking a deep breath, I began toward the train station, and as luck would have it, the first of my trains was just arriving at the station and I quickly hopped aboard.

During the ride, I thought about a decent motorbike I'd seen for sale near my house and wondered about its current availability. That would be my first stop before the gym tomorrow.

Slowly the train arrived at Central Station, and I got off to catch the second train that would take me home. The station was still brimming with a few tourists here and there I easily weaved through, along with the few locals and homeless who sat on the edges of the floor in hopes of someone giving them a Euro or two.

With my mind on the black and red bike I was hoping to get my hands on, I waited on the train platform and heard a sharp scream. My head snapped up to see a woman with shock on her face as a man ran off with her bag in tow, typical Brussels.

The man was coming in my direction and I took action. With an easy leap, I tackled the short man. His body slammed against the tiled floor with a thud as I snatched the shockingly heavy bag from him and tossed it away before my fists landed on his face the same way they'd landed in the face of my opponent earlier tonight.

It wasn't long before blood was leaking from his nose and mouth as he begged me to stop. Maybe the rage from having my own property stolen had come out when I saw this woman have her property snatched from her hands by some low-life fucker.

With the sight of blood, some around began to cry out for me to stop, but what made me ultimately stop was the sound of children crying.

I was taken back to my own childhood while my father laid into my mother, beating her senseless as I was doing to this man. I was scared and the knowledge

I could be scaring these children brought me out of my rage and into the present.

I stood from the man who pulled himself from the ground bewildered, blood pouring from his face. He looked at me, fear in his wide eyes, but it served him right.

"Get the *fuck* out of here," I growled, my voice low, and menacing.

Knowing I meant business, he staggered away as quickly as he could manage, blood leaving a trail from where I'd kicked his ass.

The dark gray duffle bag he'd snatched from the woman lay near. Bending, I picked it up by the strap and stepped in her direction. The crowd began to part to allow me through to where she stood, her deep brown eyes filled with gratefulness as I handed the bag over.

"Me… Merci," she stuttered nervously as she took the bag back with a shaky hand. She was clearly in shock from the entire incident.

I peered down at the soft pink embroidery on the bag. There was a name, *Nina*.

"De rien," it wasn't a problem taking care of the weak punk who'd made it his business to take advantage of her.

My eyes took her in. She was thin, but curvy and tall. Her dark hair was braided into long individual braids that went down her back. The dark skin of her bare shoulders was like a smooth dark chocolate bar with not a flaw in sight. There was a sensuality about her curves as she stood in all black with plump lips and delicately sweet hooded brown eyes. She was honestly the most beautiful woman I'd ever had the chance to rest my eyes on. She was one of those women I'd remember until the day I entered my own grave. Perfection.

That moment in time struck me. This wasn't by chance. It was on purpose.

CHAPTER TWO

NINA

I'd let my guard down. I didn't know how. I grew up watching my surroundings and knowing exactly what was up and who the shady perps were. I grew up in Brussels and I knew all the risks. I'd seen it done plenty of times too. Tonight, after a tiring performance, I'd lost myself in my own head, in my own fears, and in my pulsing anxiety.

Every day was a battle with my anxiety, but as specific dates neared, it was easy to lose the control I'd gained. Like smoke slipping through fingers, my resolve was slipping, and my panic settled in deeper.

As fast as my bag was snatched off my arm in the crowded station, a white knight was quick to my rescue. The guy who'd not just gotten my bag back but beat the shit out of the guy who'd taken it in the first place was a beast of a man. He stood next to me, tall and bulging. The tight dark gray shirt he wore left nothing to the imagination and I turned away trying not to gawk.

With my limbs jittering, my breaths were hurried and sweat filled my palms. I fought with my focus, but I was losing it quickly with the last couple minutes replaying in my mind repeatedly. My own mistakes the most prominent in my mind.

"Nina, are you okay?" The stranger who'd saved my bag asked.

I hadn't realized I was hyperventilating and shaking so intensely. With the racing of my heart, I felt like I'd completely lost control which only made it worse. I shook my head at his question.

"Where do you live? I can take you home."

"Jette," I managed to tell him.

"Perfect, me too." He gave me a warm smile and even though I didn't know him, it was comforting, the racing of my heart began to slow, and the churning of my stomach settled. I was grateful to the stranger who took it upon himself to take care of me. "Je m'appelle, Marc."

"Merci, Marc," my voice sounded small in comparison to his deep tone.

Wait.

It struck me he was a complete stranger that knew my name. It was strange only until I glanced down and saw it where it's always been on my bag.

We waited side by side on the station platform in silence. There were whispers and eyes staring us down after Marc's assault on the man who tried to take my bag. As if he sensed the attention we were already being given, he wrapped his strong, muscular arm around my exposed shoulder.

"It's okay."

I peered up at him and gave him a weak smile. With each passing moment of having him near, my anxiety lessened and eased. The only other natural thing which had that effect on my anxiety was dance. Dance kept me alive and kept me as sane as it possibly could.

Growing up as a black immigrant in a largely white country wasn't the easiest. Technically, I wasn't an immigrant, just the first of my family born in Europe, but still inferior to my white counterparts. As a teenager, my love for ballet saved my life, literally. It pulled me from the dark and lonely depths and breathed life into me.

With the train arriving, Marc kept his arm around me, and we boarded together. There was a single seat and Marc led me to it. I sat with my bag on my lap while Marc stood next to me, holding the pole.

Timidly, I glanced up at the man and took in his massive body. He obviously worked out and did so frequently and with apparent dedication. From where I was sitting, it was hard to miss the bulge in his dark sweatpants. I peered away so as to not get caught staring at his crotch, but looked back and allowed my eyes to scan higher over his clearly muscular chest and arms to his gorgeous blue eyes and bald head.

His eyes met mine and I quickly looked away with my cheeks heated. He was handsome as all hell, but at a time like this, I shouldn't have been thinking about how delicious he looked. He was still a complete stranger who'd I'd just witnessed beat the absolute shit out of a guy and was now escorting me home.

Eventually, the person next to me got off the train and Marc took the seat. He peered down at my bag that had been stolen from me briefly. Just thinking about it sent my heart racing again. I couldn't afford to lose the contents of my bag.

"What's in the bag anyway? A million Euros?" Marc gave me a playful nudge that made me smile.

I shook my head simply.

"Just my gear but it's fairly expensive," I unzipped my bag and reached in to pull out a pair of powdered blush pointe shoes. "I make my living with these. They are kind of necessary."

The train came to a stop and I glanced up to see my stop. I rose and Marc stood with me as we got off the train together. I led the way out of the station, across the dimly lit parking lot, and onto the street. We strolled together innocently, the dimness of the streetlights lighting our path.

"You're a dancer," he spoke for the first time since we got off the train.

"Oui. I dance and teach dance at the conservatory. It's my passion. Not many people understand." I shrugged. It was a fact of my life most didn't understand how dance filled me, nor the emotions it evoked. Being on stage or with my students displaying my passion kept me from my darker moments.

"I understand. It's not easy to explain how something that seems simple to others can make you feel whole. I'm an MMA fighter," Marc explained.

I smiled up at him.

He understood in a way nobody had before. "That's my place there." He quickly pointed out a modernly designed apartment building I remembered being remodeled about a year back.

"MMA. That explains the ass-kicking you gave that guy back at the station," I commented in a matter-of-fact tone as I hugged my black, off the shoulder sweater around my body.

"A little," Marc gave a laugh and peered down at me as we turned the corner and arrived in front of a modest brick apartment building.

"This is home," I nodded to the building I'd stopped in front of. "Merci beaucoup. I honestly mean it. You didn't have to do this for me. I'm sure you have a family waiting for you to get home."

"No family, just me, and I get it. Sometimes I get where my heart races and I can't breathe. It's not fun but we have to deal with it. Bonsoir." With a wave, Marc turned away from me.

I watched him for a moment before I produced my keys and began to unlock the front door of my building.

"Hey, if you want to come to the gym. You can check it out. A body like yours, you'd be a good fighter. We've got a few women. How about it?"

Turning back to him, I saw the hope I might take

the chance at coming to check out the gym he fought at. I didn't quite know about that, but there was this bit of desire in the back of my mind to see him again.

"Umm, je ne sais pas."

"How about you come with me and just check the place out?" This guy didn't give up. I liked his attitude. I didn't want to seem too eager and say *yes*, but I definitely didn't want to say *no*.

"When?" I stood in a relaxed stance, my hands on my hips as I tried my best not to appear wound up over his proposition.

"Tomorrow afternoon. I've got some business to handle in the morning but tomorrow afternoon I can pick you up." It was an offer I didn't want to refuse.

Normally, I wasn't one to jump at a chance like this. I considered myself reserved except when I was on stage giving it my all. Something in the back of my mind whispered to me this wasn't by chance. There was a purpose to the madness of the universe, I believed that wholeheartedly.

"Okay."

"Perfect. I'll be here hopefully around une heure moins quart. Is that okay?"

"Its good."

"Bonsoir et à demain."

Once again, he bid me goodnight and turned away leaving me smiling. I finished unlocking the door and stepped into the foyer of my building. Unlocking the second door, I went about my usual and took the elevator upstairs. The entire time I was moving on autopilot while my mind stayed on the man who I'd only known for a short time but had intrigued me deeply. He talked about dealing with anxiety, from the outside looking in, I'd never expect him to deal with anxiety the way I had. He was different but in a good way.

I SAT on my couch nervously awaiting Marc's arrival and glanced down at my smartphone. It was twelve fifty-five. He was ten minutes late, but he did say he'd be around twelve forty-five and it wasn't a definite time. Rubbing my hands together, I tried to silence the negative voices that crept into my mind with every passing moment of his tardiness.

Those voices had always been with me. They kept the constant reminder I wasn't good enough or didn't belong. I fought to keep my confidence and those voices generally came to tear me down.

They took on different people in my life—from my strict mother to my strong-willed father. There was my grandmother, and my brother every now and then. Old classmates and teachers would come through to torture me and scare me out of what I wanted. The harshest would be that of my ex-husband whom I kept buried deep in the confines of my mind under contents to never be allowed free but on occasion he'd leap into my mind and release his horror on me.

"You don't mean nothing to those white people," my dad

would say in his thick African accent when I'd express wanting to spend time with my friends who were born and bred Belgians. *"Do you think those white people would die for you? Eh? Do you think they care what happens to you?"*

Growing up in an immigrant family was hard. I was the first member of my immediate family to be born in Europe. My parents fled violence in Mali in 1990 while my mother was pregnant with me. It was the two of them with my older brother, Jaheem. They struggled to make their way but eventually, my father found a job driving taxis, while my mother cleaned houses.

Later my father's mother, my grandmother, joined my aunt, uncle, and their three children. It was family above all else but none of them understood me, I was different. I stood out and had adapted to European life. My struggle was different from theirs and my Belgian counterparts. It gave me uncertainty, fear, anxiety, and overwhelming depression.

My eyes fluttered down to my wrist where two of the many scars were visible. Swallowing hard, I shoved my sleeve down over them. They were my pain, my deliverance, and my secret.

The buzz alerting me to a guest downstairs pulled me out of my thoughts. Those were some of the thoughts I danced to keep away. I didn't want to slip. I wouldn't be able to afford another slip into the abyss of my depression.

Standing from my couch, I spotted myself in a mirror. We *were* going to the gym after all. I dressed in a dark purple pair of leggings with a pink tank top and jacket that matched my pants. My braids were pulled back in a low ponytail.

"J'arrive," I said into the intercom in my apartment before I grabbed my small purse from my dining room table and pulled the long strap over my shoulder.

With a deep breath, I left my apartment behind. Taking the stairwell down, I tried not to hurry too quickly down the stone stairs to the foyer. I paced myself, taking relatively relaxed steps as my heart beat out of my chest wildly.

I reached the ground floor, turned the corner, and there he was standing in the foyer looking even more handsome than last night. He stood waiting in dark gray sweatpants and a gray hoodie. The smile on his face brightened as he caught sight of me. In the daylight, I was able to make out the brightness of his eyes better. They were stunningly striking, like the shallows of the Mediterranean.

"Bonjour," he removed his hood before giving me the traditional kiss on the cheek greeting.

"Bonjour," I greeted him as I stood back, awaiting what was next.

"Let's go. I'm parked out front. You might need this," he handed me something I hadn't noticed him holding in the first place, a silver motorcycle helmet. As he turned toward the door, I froze in my tracks before he turned back to me and with a sly grin and winked. "You'll be fine, promise."

I trusted him.

Following Marc, we left the building and I saw parked out front was a sleek black and red motorcycle. It wasn't a rumbling Harley but one of those sporty ones that made a loud humming noise as it sped through the neighborhood.

"I had a silver one. It was stolen last night," Marc explained as we reached his new bike. "I bought this one this morning."

"Wow," I checked out the fast bike. I'd never ridden a motorcycle before.

"Come on." Marc put his helmet over his head, and I followed suit. He mounted the bike and motioned for me to follow suit.

Nervously, I swung my leg over the bike and climbed on behind him. Instinctively, my arms went around his waist to keep myself from falling off. I shuddered at the feel of his hard abs under my fingertips. Who exactly was this man? He was nothing like I'd encountered before and he was yanking me from my comfort zone while I tagged along in a way so unlike my reserved self.

"You'll be fine, ma petite danseuse. Just hold on tight," his muffled voice called. *His* Little Dancer, I inhaled deeply at the nickname as I gripped him tighter.

With a rumbling zoom, we were off. Buildings passed by at a rapid pace. Darting toward a busy intersection, I shut my eyes tightly and held on to Marc tighter as if it was possible.

Marc brought the bike to a stop.

I peeled my eyes open to find us waiting at the stoplight. The tenseness in my limbs just relaxed before the light was green and we were off again. It was a new way to see the city I worked in, danced in, and called home.

We zipped and zagged through traffic in the underground tunnels of Brussels. I nervously giggled at the mix of terror and elation which entrapped my body. The recklessness of it all was addicting and with each passing moment, I wanted more.

Arriving in the municipality of Ixelles, and the neighborhood I knew well, Matongé, Marc parked his bike in an alleyway. I swung my leg to get off the motorbike, tumbling slightly at a misstep when Marc grabbed me around my waist and steadied me.

"M… Mer… Merci," I stammered in embarrassment, my limbs tense to keep myself from shaking under his touch.

"Ça va?" Marc asked, concern in his voice as his arm stayed looped around my waist holding me upright and close to him.

"Oui, ça va," I anxiously answered.

Slowly, Marc's arm loosened and my limbs relaxed as he took a step back. Yet, I instantly wanted him closer again, feeling the heat of his body searing me with its intensity.

Watching him take off his helmet, I remembered my own and quickly removed mine and handed it over to him.

Marc gave me a subtle wink with a charmingly

mischievous smile as he took the helmet and secured both to the bike.

"Come with me," he instructed with a nod toward the street.

He motioned for me to walk ahead out of the alley into the vibrancy that was Matongé. The neighborhood known for being mostly Congolese, was a dynamic mix of African cultures I'd spent a lot of time in growing up. When my parents had first moved to Belgium, they made immediate connections with the other Africans in the neighborhood.

With Marc by my side, we strolled down the block, and past quite a few shops I knew which catered to Africans and those with a love or connection to the largest continent on Earth. This was where we could find products only found back home, stylists for our hair, good African food, and community.

For me though, I had never truly molded with any of the other Africans I met. I was the child of immigrants, but had taken on an identity molded by the country I was born in. Yet, I didn't fit in completely with those of my home country.

"It's just there," Marc pointed out an inconspicuous doorway with a plaque on the door that read, *Jean De Smet - Mixed Martial Arts Gym*. "It's upstairs."

I followed Marc up the stairs. As we reached the halfway point, I began to hear the grunts of people fighting, the smack of gloves against punching bags, and the shouting of a coach challenging all of them. Along with the sounds came the smell of pure sweat.

This wasn't the foul smell one had to deal with on the crowded metro on a hot day, but the scent of hard work.

At the top of the stairs, I gaped at the sight in front of me. It was like a scene from a sports movie. Each of the large punching bags had someone throwing punches at it. All of them lost in their own worlds as they fought their leather opponents.

In the back of the room was a boxing ring but it wasn't a traditional ring. This was an odd shape with a cage around it. Inside the cage were two opponents, both women who were throwing punches and dodging them. A coach stood outside shouting instructions as they fought. I stood mesmerized as I watched them use their bodies in such a unique way. The way their feet hopped and slid around reminded me of dancing. It was an art.

"Viens avec moi." Marc took my hand. His was rough to the touch but held mine gently as he began to pull me with him past the rows of punching bags to the last one, which was empty.

Unlike the other bags, which were black, this one was bright red and a thick script in bright yellow read, *The Belgian Beast*.

"The Belgian Beast," I ran my finger along the text and the smooth leather of the bag. "Qui est-ce?" I turned to Marc intrigued.

"C'est moi," he shoved his chest out proudly and nodded to the wall nearest to us.

I hadn't noticed it and couldn't believe I'd missed it.

From top to bottom the red painted wall held a plethora of framed articles, and championship belts proudly displayed.

Stepping to the wall, my eyes scanned over the many framed newspaper clippings.

THE BELGIAN BEAST WINS AGAIN.

THERE'S NO WINNING AGAINST THE BELGIAN BEAST.

THE BELGIAN BEAST TAKES ON THE MURDERER OF MOLDOVA & TAKES THE PRIZE.

THE MMA'S CHAMPION, THE BELGIAN BEAST, RETAINS TITLE.

THE BELGIAN BEAST REMAINS UNDEFEATED.

THEY WENT ON AND ON. The black and white photos of Marc stood out in contrast to the red wall. He wasn't just some fighter, but one of the best. Turning back toward him, I could see the pride in his stance as he watched me.

"You're a big deal," I noted casually as I stepped up to him.

"He's the biggest deal, Mademoiselle," a voice joined us. A short man with a big smile stood next to Marc. He reached his arm and gave Marc a pat on the shoulder. "Recruiting, I see," he noted in Dutch.

"A little, you could say," Marc answered with a chuckle before he turned to me and switched back to

French. "Nina, this is Jean, the owner of the gym. He's also my trainer and manager."

"Lovely to meet you, young lady. Are you looking to join the world of MMA?" Jean extended his hand to me. I shook it politely.

"Marc invited me. I'm just checking it out, I suppose," I answered him shyly. Meeting new people was always incredibly awkward for me. I wasn't like my cousins who were all incredibly outgoing and social. I normally needed time to warm up to people. Marc though had been an exception to my usual rules.

"I'm going to show her a few things. I think you could use them after last night, hm?" Marc winked at me.

My cheeks flushed and I was grateful my dark skin hid the heat in my face. I was embarrassed at the events of last night and slightly infatuated with the man who saved me.

"I better get back to getting these girls in shape for their fight. Marc's a good teacher and obviously a champion who learned from the best." Jean pointed at himself boastfully.

Marc laughed and slapped the older man on the back before he jogged off to continue coaching the two girls in the odd shaped ring.

I glanced from the ring to Marc who was wrapping his hands with tape. I stood in awe of the large man who held championship titles. He wasn't like anyone else I'd met before. His exterior didn't match what I was learning about the interior and he easily connected with me, which no one ever did. Marc was different.

"What shape is the ring? It's not a square," I commented.

"It's an octagon. It's one of the things that makes mixed martial arts unique. We fight in the octagon, and we mix various styles of martial arts with other traditional fighting sports like boxing. You can really go anywhere with it and no fight is ever the same. You might be against an opponent with a background deeper in kickboxing or Muay Thai, boxing or Brazilian Jiu-Jitsu. It's a mixed bag and that's what makes it fun," Marc explained as he took my hand into his. A distinct shiver ran from the tips of my fingers, up my arm, and down my spine at his touch.

"Whore. That's all you've always been. A slutty whore." The voice that pierced loudly through my head shocked me.

I snatched my hand from Marc and wrapped my arms around myself. I hated when he came out. I tried to keep his nasty words locked inside but they always found the most inconvenient moment to burst through.

"Hey," Marc's voice broke through. "Ça va?"

My eyes found his and a solace I wasn't back in that place. I wasn't in that dingy apartment being spoken to like a common sewer rat. No longer was I suffering at the hands of a fierce abuser I thought I'd never escape. I allowed a breath free.

"Oui," I breathed. "Ça va."

"It's okay," Marc gave a reassuring smile as he took my hand back into his and gently began to wrap my knuckles with tape. "I get them too. The voices of my past that tell me I'm not good enough. They tell me I'm a loser or a piece of shit. I get them but I refuse to listen to them. Don't listen, okay?"

"Okay."

From that moment, I was bonded with this stranger. He shared one of my secrets and knew how to comfort me as if I'd known him my whole life, as if we were connected not by chance, but by purpose.

CHAPTER THREE

MARC

Nina was unique in her own way. Quiet yet expressive, dainty yet a fighter, and beyond fucking gorgeous.

I couldn't keep my eyes off her as we worked together, and any time I got to touch her was a moment to slow time down.

I instructed her on throwing a proper punch. She wasn't bad at all and her limber body helped her quickly learn how to dodge punches.

We stood in the octagon, toe to toe and she moved with such ease I was hypnotized.

"Aie," I hissed as a jab landed on my arm. I spotted a sly smile cross her lips. She'd taken advantage of my entranced state and snuck in a hit. "Very good," I congratulated her on a job well done. "You're doing good. You can be winning fights in no time."

"Does the Belgian Beast have a new opponent?" A voice came from beyond the cage.

I sharply turned in the direction of the voice and spotted a man rolling up in a wheelchair. "Will the winning streak end?"

"Never," I boasted before turning back toward Nina who watched my interaction with my old friend. "We can take a break. Get some water and we can do a cool down in a few minutes."

"Okay," her small voice answered as we strolled to the entrance of the cage together.

I placed a hand on her shoulder, she tensed under my touch but quickly relaxed as we paused, her eyes found mine instantly and I gave her a reassuring smile. She anxiously smiled back before she turned away and we continued out of the cage together.

I watched Nina stroll toward the water fountain as I jogged down the stairs and toward my friend. With dark skin like Nina and dreadlocks pulled back in a ponytail, Fabumi Omenuko was one of my oldest friends. We used to train and fight together until Fabumi suffered an injury in the octagon that left him confined to a wheelchair.

"What's up?" I approached him and bent down, giving him a hug.

"Nothing, brother. Just thought I'd stop by and congratulate you on your latest win. Still undefeated," he noted proudly.

"Always undefeated, and don't forget it, fucker," I proclaimed with a grin as I leaned against the metal fencing of the cage.

Fabumi laughed. He had this loud booming laugh

that took up the space in a room. There was a while where that laugh had faded. After that fateful night, my friend was paralyzed from the waist down, he couldn't find joy in anything in life, but after a while that joy came back as he found a new purpose, his beautiful wife.

Fabumi's laughter died down and he glanced around the place that used to be a second home to him.

"Who's the girl?" He nodded toward Nina who stood with a bottle of water, her eyes examining the red wall of dedication to myself and the success I'd brought to the gym.

I shrugged off his question and he raised his eyebrows at me and grinned.

"You like her? She's new here?"

"All these questions," I commented casually in hopes he'd lay off. My eyes caught her once more. Her body moved with an easy grace that captured me easily.

"Yeah, you like her. Where's she from?" Fabumi was back to his line of questioning and I hadn't even answered the first one.

"I only met her last night."

"Last night? At the fight?"

"No. I was on my way home and some fucker tried to snatch her bag at Central Station. I beat the fuck out of the perp and then escorted her home. She only lives about a block from me. I invited her to come hang out and learn a few self-defense tactics," I explained to my friend.

"And you want to do the nasty with her, right?" He

raised his eyebrows and a sly smile spread across his face.

"I only just met the girl. Fuck off. How's things with you? How's Emmy?" I worked quickly to change the subject as my face heated intensely.

Fabumi laughed loudly. "Changing the subject, I'll play along. Emmy is good. Her belly is huge, and she complains about her back all day, but all is good, just waiting on my baby boy." My friend grinned from ear to ear proudly. He and his wife were expecting their first baby very soon.

"Fabumi!" Jean's jubilant voice cheered across the gym.

I peered up to see my trainer coming across the gym.

When I joined the gym at fifteen, Fabumi was also just starting out. He was seventeen and at six-foot-two, he was big and fierce. We trained with one another and made each other stronger. Our bond formed immediately and when he was injured, I nearly left the sport, my heart broken, but I continued for him.

"Mon fils!" Jean beamed as he slapped Fabumi on the shoulder. "Ça va, mon fils?"

"Ça va," Fabumi answered to the man who'd been a father figure to the both of us since we were teenagers.

"Is the baby here yet?" Jean excitedly asked.

"No, but soon," Fabumi told him.

I shifted my attention away from their conversation and my eyes found Nina sipping her water.

Her pouted lips over the bottle.

I licked my own lips watching her.

"This one is over here about to surrender it all," Fabumi joked as he slapped my arm. I snapped back to reality and into the conversation with my friend and trainer. "You've got it bad for that girl. I think you need to make your next move."

"Next move?" I shrugged as I dismissed him.

"A date, and not to the gym, dumbass." He was matter of fact.

"She does seem like a nice girl," Jean added. I rolled my eyes at the men and lifted a hand to dismiss them before stepping away.

I strolled toward Nina who still stood at the wall. Her fingers hovered over one of my championship belts. My eyes peered over her body, her curves were so defined and perfect to me. Her body toned beyond the average woman because of her dancing.

"I won that one nearly a year ago."

She jumped at my voice and turned back to me, her hand over her chest.

"Je suis désolé, I didn't mean to scare you."

"Do you have to defend your championship?"

"Oui, in a couple months. That's my next big fight."

"Good luck."

"Thanks." I gave her a smile. "You did good today. You have natural abilities. Some people come in here and we have to really teach them, but it came natural to you."

"Thanks, but I think I'll stick to the stage," she shrugged as she peered at me through her deliciously long lashes. Every time she looked at me with her sensual brown eyes it was hard to swallow. She took my breath away easily. "I'm exhausted."

The sound of her stomach growling made her jump and she covered her stomach with her hands and glanced away embarrassed.

"And hungry. Me too. Do you want to grab something?"

"Umm, sure."

"Let's get this tape off our hands and get going. I know just the place."

———

IT WAS one of those rare occasions where the Belgian weather held nicely, and it wasn't too windy or cold even for September. I sat across from Nina at an outside table at a Turkish kebab snack bar not far from the gym that was a typical haunt of mine after a good workout.

"You like?" I questioned before popping a frite in my mouth.

"Mmmhmm," she hummed her answer and nodded, her mouth full of food. Her lips curled into a grin before she took a bite into her durum wrap. She chewed and swallowed. "I don't normally eat like this, but I was starving."

"Sometimes a little junk food hits the spot." I winked in her direction.

She nodded enthusiastically as she took another

bite. With each moment I spent with her, she came to life a little more.

Nina guarded herself. I used to be the same. I locked myself away. I was already getting hurt enough at home, I didn't need someone else hurting me too. Even after joining the gym, it took me awhile to open up and once I did, my life drastically changed. To have positive influences and people in my life immediately turned it around. She needed support like I got, she obviously didn't have it. I wanted to give it to her.

"When do you dance?" I asked, intrigued about her dance career.

"I teach most days of the week. Today is my day off."

I kept a note in my mind she was off on Fridays. "I perform at least twice a week, sometimes more depending on the schedule. I practice four or five days a week depending on the schedule. It's my life."

Her entire face lit up as she spoke about her career. She loved dance with everything inside her. It seemed to be what kept her going.

"How long have you been dancing?"

"Since I was five. My mom signed me up as an after-school activity and I couldn't stop. It was the one thing I had in life that I was completely connected to. I've only ever stopped once and I regret it," she expressed a sadness with having stopped dancing.

"Why?"

"Life."

A darkness came over us with her answer. The smile on her face faded quickly and the air around us stilled. I could almost hear the thumping of her heart across the table. Being smart, I wouldn't push her for more information which was hers to reveal at her own time.

"I'll have to come see you perform one day. I'm curious. I've never been to the ballet before." I allowed a small chuckle to lighten the air around us, and I clearly heard her breathe a sigh of relief at me not asking further questions.

"You must. It's such a wonderful experience. I wish my family would come more often. They tend to stay away from that part of my life. It's not really them," she expressed.

"Same for me. The fighting is a little much for my family. I wish they could come more, but I understand." I gave her a reassuring grin to show her I understood.

"Who was the guy in the wheelchair?" she asked.

I laughed. "Just Fabumi. He's a good friend of mine and used to be a fighter. I don't know if you've noticed but the sport is dangerous. Injuries happen and sometimes you can't be healed from them. He ended up with a spinal injury that left him paralyzed."

Nina gaped before she covered her mouth.

"Wow, I'm sorry for your friend," she said in utter shock.

I shrugged easily as Fabumi did when he addressed his condition. It had been his life for five years and as the years passed, he was able to not just accept it but shrug it off.

"He'll be fine," I commented as I watched Nina's

eyes widened, but before words could leave my mouth, my shoulders were grabbed sharply, and I felt the blade of a knife at the side of my neck.

"Don't move, klootzak," a gruff and dark voice said directly in my ear. I knew exactly who it was and sighed. Sophie had gotten herself in a bind once again.

"If anyone is a ball sack, it's you, Bart," I hissed, careful to not move my head too much and get a blade to the neck.

The panic in Nina's eyes was telling and to keep her calm, I kept my cool with the men I'd come in contact with many times. Bart's grip on me tightened when I'd insulted him back. He was just one of the low-lifes my sister got herself tangled up with.

"Shut the fuck up," he hissed angrily as he pressed the knife to my neck a little more. I could just feel the blade nicking at my skin. "Your sister owes me and seems to have skipped out on me. That little bitch."

"How much, Bart?" These guys didn't scare me. Their tactics worked on others and sure as fuck worked on my sister but not me.

I knew she'd run off for a reason. Sophie and her inherited addiction to gambling. My dad would say, *"De appel valt niet ver van de boom."* The funny thing was that he would refer to me but the apple that didn't fall far was my sister. She took after him in his worst ways. She hydrated on alcohol and got her high from gambling away all her money, sometimes mine, and many times the man of dangerous men, like Bart, who wanted it returned with interest.

"She took two thousand from me. I want back three," Bart demanded with a sneer.

Nina let out a whimper.

I looked at her until her eyes met mine. I conveyed my relaxed nature through my eyes to calm her. She swallowed hard and her eyes never left mine. I had to reassure her she was okay with me and nothing would happen to her.

"Done," I answered Bart easily as I reached into my pocket and produced my wallet. Taking a stack of mostly green and some orange and blue Euro bills, I counted out three-thousand Euros before shoving the stack of money at him. "Here's your money, now leave me and my friend the fuck alone. If you have business with my sister, fucking find her. I have nothing to do with your shit."

I stood and turned to the man I could finally see for the first time. With my height, I easily towered over the man who gaped at me with wide eyes. I took a step in his direction and he nearly tripped over the corner of a chair. One of his goons grabbed him and quickly stabilized him.

"Now get the fuck out of here," I growled angrily as I punched my fist against my other hand. At the sound of my fist hitting skin, Bart and his little sidekick jumped before turning and rushing away up the street without another word. "Fuckers," I hissed as I sat back at the table.

Nina was shaking and I could see tears forming in

the corners of her eyes. Fuck, those guys had to ruin something good for me.

"Hey, it's okay," I took her hand into mine and rubbed the back of her hand with my thumb. I was used to that kind of shit, but it didn't mean she was. It wasn't exactly normal to be approached on the street and to have someone put a knife to your neck. "I'm really sorry about that. My sister gets herself into some fucked up shit and big brother is always bailing her out as you can see."

She sniffed to keep her tears at bay, and I continued to hold her hand.

Flipping her hand over, I allowed my fingers to playfully tap and massage the inside of her hand until a smile slowly began to grace her lips. That's all I wanted.

"Do you have siblings?" I asked as my index finger traced the lines of her hand.

"An older brother. He's pretty protective, like you."

"We've got to be sometimes. My sister, I love her to death, but I just wish she wouldn't get into so much shit. Maybe one day but that's a pretty big wish."

"She's lucky to have a brother like you."

"I hope she feels that way." My fingers walked along her hand pulling a giggle from her. Wow, that laugh was something else and I instantly wanted to hear its harmonic tone again. My fingers got to work again tickling along her hand and over her wrist until my eyes landed on a scar. There was actually more than one along her wrist.

Nina's eyes widened as she snatched her hand away and shoved the sleeve of her jacket over her wrist.

"You okay?"

"I'm fine," she shot defensively before she abruptly stood from her seat. "Umm, thanks for the lesson and for lunch. It was nice of you. I should really get going. My family gets together on Fridays. Au revoir." Then she was off up the street.

I gaped at her unable to process what happened.

She'd walked away and I wanted so much more time with her. I feared that was all the time I'd get.

CHAPTER FOUR

NINA

He'd seen my secret. The one thing I kept guarded and close to me. "I didn't want anyone to know the pain I inflicted upon my life, and the strength it took me to rid myself from the world of hurt." With walking away, I blew my chances at getting to know more about the stranger who understood me in more ways than one and had broken me out of my sheltered shell.

Back inside my shell I went as I finished tying my scarf on my head and straightened the sleeves of my top. It was Friday after all, and that meant a special kind of torture I endured once a week, time with my family.

It was Jumah, the day of gathering, and like every Friday in my Muslim family, we were all expected to make an appearance. Mom always made sure to cook everyone's favorites to lure us to the family home. I knew if I didn't come, she'd spend the next week blowing up my phone and wouldn't let me live it down. Family was the most important part of life to her.

Leaving my apartment, I was afraid he'd be there, waiting for me with questions, but he wasn't. It was business as usual in the neighborhood with children riding bikes after school, friends strolling and chatting, and stay-at-home moms with strollers holding adorable little babies. There was no Marc and if I was brave enough to admit it, I was disheartened at his absence.

I took the train as normal, but this time I had to change trains to leave the city altogether. During my final year of secondary school, my parents decided to leave Brussels behind for the Flemish city of Halle. It wasn't as fast paced as the city and I think my parents thought leaving the city would urge me to connect more with my familiar roots, but I only wanted to run away more and dive deeper into dance.

My knuckles knocked at my parents' door as usual. I'd been on autopilot and hadn't paid much attention the entire way to their house but was caught in my overflowing mind as usual.

"Nina!" My mother gushed as she swung the door open. She looked the same as usual, her dark skin illuminated against the bright yellow of her dress and headscarf. The wrinkles around her eyes seemed to grow with each visit as she aged. She was still just as beautiful but exhausted as she'd hung up her housekeeping apron for the role of grandma to my brother's four children. "I just finished the Jollaf rice."

Always making my favorites to keep me coming back. It was generally the one day of the week I splurged on foods I didn't eat frequently. I needed to keep in shape for dance after all.

"Bonjour Maman," I greeted my mother as she ushered me anxiously into the house.

Her hands grabbing my arms at random to feel if I'd gotten any meat on my bones. The scents of Africa spilled out from the kitchen and the sounds of children filled the halls.

Family brought it all together the way Mom liked it, and on our day of prayer all of us were expected to break bread together and thank Allah.

"When was the last time you ate?" My mother squeezed my arm tightly.

I sighed. In some families you were picked on because you were overweight, but in mine I was the object of humiliation for being thin. My mom never let me live it down and I was constantly encouraged to eat as if I didn't live a perfectly healthy lifestyle.

"Maman, I'm fine," I grumbled in annoyance at my mother's jabbing.

She ignored my clear irritation and continued about me being skin and bones and how I should eat more or come over more often for good homemade meals. Giving up as I tended to do every week, her words fell on deaf ears.

"There's ma petite soeur!" I was greeted immediately upon entering the back veranda of my parent's home.

My brother stood with open arms and a huge smile on his face.

I smiled at the man who was my first friend. As children, we only had one another and eventually our cousins who joined the family in Europe later.

Jaheem was five years older than me. He immigrated with my parents and held memories of our homeland. Sometimes he and our parents would reminisce together about their days in Mali while I was left out, having never been until I was much older, and while for them it was a return home, for me it was taking a step into a strange land I felt no physical connection with.

"Mon grand frère." As I reached him, I threw my arms around him and he picked me up. I giggled loudly as my big brother did what he tended to do every week. It was a tradition.

"Put her down, she could get hurt!" Our mother fussed as she'd done since we were children.

"That's right. You already know she's tiny, don't want to break her," a voice interrupted my giggles and I peered over to my sister-in-law, Jaheem's wife, Suzanna.

I wouldn't call her my best friend, or my enemy. Suzanna and I got along the one time a week I saw her, and that was the extent of our relationship. She was the ideal African woman with flawless deep skin, and an incredibly shapely body from a huge chest to wide hips that grew with each child she and my brother produced. I was a beanstalk compared to her, but I was proud of the curves I did possess.

"Bonjour, Suzanna," I greeted her as my brother put me down. I bent and kissed her cheek followed by the forehead of the toddler sleeping in her lap. The little boy's lips were pursed as he slumbered away in his mother's arms.

"Bonjour," Suzanna greeted me with no particular emotion and I was fine with that.

Suzanna was originally from Mali's neighboring country Burkina Faso. She always seemed a little high strung to me and we never particularly took time to know one another. My brother loved her, and she was the type of good Muslim girl my parents wanted him with. They married as soon as my brother finished university and got to making babies right away. There were four all together. The baby in Suzanna's arms and the other three off in the other room likely murdering one another without adult supervision as Jaheem and I normally did as children.

"Où est Papa?" I realized my father was nowhere to be seen.

"Imam asked for some handyman help after prayer and you know your father is the number one handyman and always ready to help," Mom noted as she returned to the warm veranda with a bowl in hand. She handed it directly to me and the scent of the rice floated into my nostrils.

My favorite, *riz au gras or* Jollof rice. With just the smell, I could already taste the curry spices on my tongue and my mouth was watering. Her food was always a weakness and would continue to be.

Taking my seat with my bowl, the doorbell rang, and mom was back toward the door. This was how every Friday went and I both enjoyed and despised it at the same time. As I dug into my dish, family members began to flood into the room. My aunt and uncle strolled in with my grandmother and two of my cousins.

My cousin Arjana strolled with two babies on her hips and her third trailing behind. Her husband was usually late as he arrived after work. Then there was my cousin Ayodele or Ayo for short. Of everyone in my family, he and I were the absolute closest. Ayo was a year old when arriving in Belgium and though he had the smallest connection to home, he didn't have memories to depend on like everyone else.

As usual, grandma took her seat. She wouldn't move much for the rest of the evening, but at eighty-six nobody expected her to. I stood and greeted her, my aunt and uncle, then Arjana before Ayo threw his arms around me.

"Ma chouchoutte," he gushed as usual before he let go of me and I took my seat with him next to me. "Without fail your mother has got you with the rice."

"Of course, she has," I drawled to Ayo's laughter.

"In her hopes that it goes straight to those lean dancer hips of yours."

It was all true. Mom thought fattening me up was the key to achieving her end goal of me settling down again and this time producing a few grandchildren for her. "I swear. These women and their demands of us."

Like me, Ayo didn't connect with our usual family goals, traditions, and dare I say it, values. I'd once walked down the path of doing what the family wanted, I gave up the life I wanted for what they saw as admirable. I'd bent to their will, but Ayo refused to be anyone but himself and though he was my younger cousin, I looked up to him for it.

"Do you know my mother had the nerve to ask me when I planned to marry a nice girl?" His voice sounded with disgust as he crossed his legs.

My poor aunt refused to see it even though Ayo had come out of the closet years ago. There would be no marrying of a nice girl for my fantastically gay cousin. I snickered in response to my cousin slapping my arm.

For my family, they would rather pretend Ayo wasn't who he adamantly said he was. They still loved him but didn't exactly accept him. It was the same with me and therefore the two of us only had one another for that complete love and acceptance of every part of ourselves.

"What's new with you?" Ayo changed the subject of our family politics. He knew the subject was touchy with me after what I'd been through.

I only supplied with him a small shrug. For the most part, everything was normal with me. I taught, went to rehearsals, and performed. It was all perfectly ordinary except for one thing, Marc. The man refused to leave my brain. I didn't know what he wanted with me in the first place, I was just some damaged girl determined to live my dreams to their fullest. Yet, he'd taken this affinity to me. I couldn't put my finger on it, nor the fact I liked it. For the first time, there was a man I'd taken a deep liking to. I craved his presence around me, I felt unnaturally safe and afraid at the same time.

"Tell me about him," my cousin demanded without me uttering a single word.

I stared at him; eyes wide. "For you to be so nonchalant, it has to be a guy. Spill the tea, sister."

"Honestly, I really don't know. The other night leaving my performance some asshole snatched my bag at Central Station. This guy comes out of nowhere and tackles the guy. He beats him up and gets my bag back for me. I was shaken up and he ended up riding with me and walking me home. Turns out he's an MMA fighter and he invited me to his gym. We worked out together and we had lunch." As I told the story to Ayo, he sat gripped on my every word as if this was the gossip of the week. I shrugged it off lightly. "He was just a nice guy who helped me out."

"But you like him?"

"Likes who?" A voice shook us from our bubble. Dad had returned home and stood right over the two of us on the couch.

"Rein," I dismissed it easily and quickly stood to hug my dad who gripped me in a tight bear hug before kissing my forehead. "Comment ça va, Papa?"

"Bien, ma petite," Dad answered and I could hear

Marc in my head and his little term of endearment for me, *ma petite danseuse*.

I would accept I'd likely never see him again.

MY EYES STUDIED the girls who danced for me. All of them teenagers, but all very advanced in the art form. This type of study didn't come cheap. I remembered my parents barely scraping together the funds to pay for my mediocre dance classes. The class I taught was much different and the parents of my students paid thousands to be taught by the best.

"Get that leg higher, Adeline," I instructed one of the girls who immediately took my instruction and positioned herself with her leg extended higher like a graceful gazelle, tall, lean, and elegant.

Dance was one of the purest forms of art in my opinion. It was completely reliant upon the body in every single way. It drove away demons and invited in only the best feelings. There was some pain, but it was a pain which held a purpose. It wasn't pain brought on by someone who wished harm but by oneself to strengthen the learned skills.

I'd been through so much pain in my life, but the most welcomed pain was brought on by dance. The bruises and scars I obtained when I danced were my proud battle scars that showed my commitment.

I had other scars though, some physical like the ones Marc saw, and then the mental ones. My self-imposed physical scars were my attempt to silence the mental ones that haunted me daily.

"That's all for today, girls. I'll see you soon." I waved off my students as the music finished. I only had a short time to get from the conservatory to the opera where tonight's performance was to take place.

Day in and day out, I lived under my rigorous schedule. It kept me busy and out of my head where my mental scars tended to keep me company, and it kept me gainfully employed.

I threw my bag over my shoulder, stepped out of the studio, and out into the chilly, drizzly air of Brussels. I grunted at the usual weather and hugged my coat around my body as I strolled the cobblestone streets toward the city's renowned opera house, La Monnaie De Munt.

Thankfully, the drizzle in the air had thinned the usual crowds of tourists that hogged the streets of the center of the city near The Grand Place and the Opera House. I arrived as usual and strolled quickly toward the backdoor of the old institution built in 1818, but was stopped in my tracks at the sight of the man I figured I'd never see again.

"Bonjour, ma petite danseuse," Marc greeted me with a sly smile and my stomach did somersaults. I had no words as my eyes studied him.

Marc stood in a sleek black tuxedo. He cleaned up nicely and was more debonair than I remembered from when I'd last seen him over a week ago. I swallowed hard.

"I thought I'd pick up a ticket to the ballet," he gave a careless shrug.

Reaching into his pocket, he pulled out a single ticket. It was to the night's performance. My heart pulsated hard in a deep thumping I felt throughout my entire body. He was coming to the show to see me perform. I'd never been nervous for a single performance until that moment.

CHAPTER FIVE

MARC

The curtains opened and a single spotlight illuminated a spot in the center of the stage where a single dancer stood on her toes. It was Nina and the light reflected gracefully off her rich, warm skin. I sat in pure awe at her poise before she began to skillfully and elegantly move across the stage, the single light following her.

I gaped at the woman who refused to leave even the smallest fucking crevices of my mind. She'd left me with so many questions and I tried to accept the cards dealt but every single morning I woke up to her face and I fell asleep to the sound of her quiet voice. All of it led me here to the ballet and watching Nina perform at what she did best.

The entire performance was more moving than I expected, and Nina was the star of it all. She captivated the audience with everything about her. She put everything into what she did, and it was obvious from her first moment on stage to the last.

When the show ended, I was the first on my feet applauding loudly as the dancers took their final bow. I spotted Nina's eyes on me before the curtain dropped and she was taken from my sight. Damn, I'd never been in awe until that moment.

"Delightful performance," a fellow patron commented as we spilled out into the square in front of the grandiose building with its large columns. I'd passed La Monnaie many times in my life, but I'd never had the opportunity, nor desire, to go inside until tonight.

Loitering, I watched as the others scattered, heading toward public transportation, taking taxis, or heading into cafes for an after-show drink. I slowly trekked through the quickly thinning crowd to the door I'd greeted Nina at as she arrived.

Members of the orchestra were exiting, their instruments in tow, all chatting with one another after their contribution to the night's performance. Following the others a few girls I recognized as some of the dancers began to exit before the one I wanted emerged, chatting with another woman before her eyes landed on me. She almost seemed to take a pause.

"I'll see you at rehearsal," Nina noted in excellent English to the women who responded the same in a thick Russian accent.

Nina hugged her arms around her body as she

approached me. She was clearly nervous with jittering limbs and biting her bottom lip.

I caught myself grinning down at her as she reached me. Nina short, but nowhere near as tall as me and I towered her thin yet noticeably curvy frame. It was something I noticed right away seeing all the dancers together on the stage, most of the girls were rail thin without any curves, but Nina was different with a clearly defined shape.

"You were fantastic. You didn't tell me you were the lead," I resounded gleefully.

Nina was the show and captured every part of the stage with the story surrounding her graceful character.

"Merci. I'm actually the understudy for the prima but she fell ill," Nina shrugged which to me undermined what she'd actually done. She was the lead, substituting or not. She owned every fucking centimeter of the stage.

"You were amazing. I'm happy I finally got to see the ballet. It was much cooler than I expected it to be," I complimented her, and she finally granted me that beautiful smile that had stayed with me since we first met.

For a moment, we stood awkwardly as Nina balanced on her heels and I tried to find words. I was never lost on words, but I didn't want to say the wrong thing. I'd already had her runaway from me once, I couldn't have that shit happen again. When I told

Fabumi what happened, he laughed at me for blowing it. I wouldn't fucking blow it again.

"J'ai faim. Es-tu?" My stomach grumbled and I swore I heard Nina's growl too as it did that day at the gym.

"Mmmhmm," she answered with a shy nod.

Inside of the shy girl that stood before me was a warrior. I'd seen it in her at the gym and more importantly I'd seen it in her eyes. Like me, Nina had obviously been through deep shit and somehow got to the other side. With that fact alone I knew she was a fighter.

"I know a place not far. How do you feel about Greek food?" I put an arm around her shoulders.

"Greek is good," she answered sweetly before pausing. "But I'm not really dressed for a restaurant," she noted as she peered down at her leggings.

I simply shrugged as I began to lead us toward the Grand Place.

"No worries, ma petite danseuse." I winked down at her only to have her shake her head with a small smile on the corner of her lips as we continued forward.

In the dim orange lights of Brussels, Nina and I strolled the old cobblestone roads together until we arrived in the world-famous Brussels Grand Place. City Hall stood before us, tall, looming, and illuminated in the darkness. A few tourists were still around snapping photos in the area that was once an old market square.

It was strange to grow up in such a place and take it

for granted. Once one took a moment to pause and enjoy the history around them, everything was so different.

I continued to lead Nina along with me until we arrived at one of the restaurants with a lucky spot in the square. A little Greek place that my mom loved called *El Greco*.

Opening the door, I allowed Nina inside the warmth of the restaurant that transported you from the drizzly European capital to the Mediterranean. The cozy atmosphere with traditional Greek music playing in the background easily set the scene.

"Bonsoir," a tanned man with a big mustache proudly greeted us.

"Bonsoir, une table pour deux s'il vous plait." I requested a table for Nina and me.

"Follow me," he instructed as we weaved through the small place and to a small table set for two in the corner. Waiting for us was a small plate with meatballs and cubes of feta cheese, this was my favorite part when my mom would bring Sophie and myself as kids.

Nina took the booth side of the table and I took the chair opposite her. She removed her coat and I caught myself gawking at her as she sat in her off the shoulder long sleeved purple shirt. The dim light of the place caught her clavicle in the perfect light, and I could already feel her collarbone under my lips as I kissed her perfect skin.

A week of thoughts like that were draining on me. Nina was this fucking mystery that my body craved, as well as my mind and spirit. She held this allure that drew me in and made it hard for me to think.

"I've never been here," Nina commented as she looked around the crowded space.

"My mom brought me and my sister here a lot when we were younger. It's her favorite. She always says in another life she was Greek." I laughed thinking of my mother who was the glue that held me in particular together. Sadly, it wasn't enough for Sophie.

"Speaking of your sister, whatever happened after those guys…?" Nina asked with pure concern after the events that took place the last time I saw her.

"Paying them off got them off my sister's back. I spoke to her. She of course thanked me through her tears and promised she'd never do it again, but that's every time. Its like a script at this point." I hated to shrug it off, but it was becoming all too fucking routine.

My biggest fear was how my sister's children would be affected by her bad decisions. She knew how our father affected us firsthand and she still followed suit.

"I'm glad things are better, for now," Nina provided a weak smile before we were approached by a waiter who took our orders before leaving the two of us once more. "You surprised me tonight."

I gave a small chuckle.

"Well, you just disappeared on me last week. I wanted to see you again. Figured the best way to do that was to see you in your own element," I confessed as she peered away bashfully.

"Wow, you make me seem so special or something," Nina appeared puzzled as the waiter delivered our drinks. Nina picked up her glass of wine and took a sip.

I was the one who was puzzled. Nina was a fascinating woman. She had this story behind her warm chocolate eyes I wanted to know more about. There was also her incredible talent that blew me away. How did she not see how special she was?

"But you are," I countered easily.

Nina only laughed before taking another sip of her drink.

"I want to get to know you, if that's okay."

"There's not much to know," she easily dismissed the notion she was someone to know better. I didn't understand how she couldn't see it. "I dance. It's my whole life really."

"You dance to hide your pain. Its like me. I fight to hide my pain. We're not much different," I told her honestly before I sipped my beer. "My father used to beat the shit out of my mother while my sister and I watched. Some days he would beat me and Sophie too. Many nights we would starve because he gambled away the money to buy us food. My life was shit growing up until I found it in myself to stand up to my father. I asserted myself as the man of the house. He died a few years later and I couldn't be happier he is off this earth. Is that terrible? Maybe, but those scars define me. I see you have some that define you too."

"I couldn't understand it. When I met you, there was this honest connection I never had with anyone else. It is like you got me and I thought it was impossible for anyone to get me after everything," she admitted.

I swear even over the chatter of the others in the restaurant, the music, and the clatter of the kitchen, I could hear her heartbeat thumping loudly.

"My family was and is loving. My parents and brother were refugees from Mali. I was born here. I was the different one. They tried to connect with me, but we never were able to on a deeper level. Dance brought me this acceptance. I was able to have something that was uniquely mine and they didn't and still don't understand."

"I can get that. For me, my mother never understood how I escaped violence by submerging myself in violence," I added thoughtfully.

Nina gave a subtle nod she understood exactly where I was coming from. "Not feeling accepted by my family nor fully by my peers gave me this pulsating anxiety that followed me and sometimes it swallowed me into depression. My parents acted as if I was making it up or being lazy, but I couldn't fight hard enough on those days. Their solution was I should get married. They thought being a devoted wife and possibly a mother one day would give me that purpose.

"Except I never found a purpose and it only made everything worse. I married the son of a family friend. His first act was to make me give up dance. He told me no self-respecting woman would show her body off the way dance did and no man who called himself a man would allow his wife to do it. He controlled every move I made from sunup to sundown. I wasn't just a prisoner to my depression, but his prisoner and the nights where he would call me names and beat me were the worst. I resorted to the only thing I knew to help deal with the pain." Nina pulled up her sleeve and there were those scars I'd seen and touched before she ran away from me.

"You cut yourself," I stated, my voice low, my hand reaching out to graze the scars over her wrist. "My sister used to do it. She might still do it. I discovered her one night when she was only about ten with a razor blade from my shaving kit." I shook my head as I was transported back to that night seeing my sister so vulnerable and desperate to strip the pain away she hurt herself to do it.

"It was all I had," Nina's voice became small and shame filled her words.

"Don't be ashamed," I laced my fingers through hers and held her hand tightly in mine. "There's no shame in dealing with pain."

"Thanks," she whispered as she took her other hand and quickly wiped away a fallen tear.

"You obviously still aren't married to him," I noted as she didn't wear a ring and she was dancing proudly.

She smiled and shook her head. "It took a lot to say enough was enough. It was the hardest decision because I knew my family would never look at me the same way. Getting a divorce isn't something we do. I come from an incredibly devout Muslim family. I wouldn't ever live down a divorce. My single act would ruin the friendship my parents held dear with his parents and I would have this mark upon me, but I did it for me. I'm proud of it even though it took a long time for my parents to really come to terms with it."

I could never imagine being held to a particular standard. That took guts of steel for Nina to do and I found myself in even more awe of her. Only her eyes showed that this woman was stronger than most muscle building fighters I knew.

"And you doubt how fucking special you are?" I questioned Nina who seemed to take my words to heart.

She sat back in her seat with a thoughtful look on her face.

My eyes roamed her visage. Her almond eyes, dimpled cheeks, and stout lips. She was sensual without trying and I was drawn to that.

"Enough about me, really," she waved her hand as if she was finished with the topic and ready to move onto something else. "You have so many belts, medals, everything. Is it true you're undefeated?"

Unlike Nina, I didn't mind being the center of attention every now and then. I'd worked hard as fuck to make myself into the icon I'd become, and I worked even harder to keep my reputation of being a stone-cold force to be reckoned with in the octagon.

Puffing out my chest, I smirked in her direction before taking a swig of my beer, leaving her in suspense at my answer.

"So, we're being coy, are we?" Nina playfully shot.

That little bit I saw in her that was joyful and fun loving was coming out and made her unique personality even more attractive. Behind it all she was just as human and broken as me, but she was able in small moments to find the laughter.

"Of course, I'm undefeated. Nobody has taken on the beast and won since I was fifteen. Not even my own fucking father could take me down once I found the fighter in me," I noted proudly.

"Seems like a lot of pressure to keep living up to that standard." She hit the nail on the head. Any fight could be the one I lost my winning streak. I fought for me and for my family. I made a name for myself and people from all over the world came to see me fight in case they were the ones to witness my downfall. I had an audience waiting for me to fail.

"It is but I take it day by day," I answered truthfully. I didn't spend much time dwelling on the possibility, but I spent my time making myself into the best I knew I could be. One day my best might be losing a fight, but that day hadn't come yet.

With our food arriving, Nina and I settled into lighter conversation. She told me about how her parents came over fleeing civil war in Mali and later more of her family followed. I told her about my upcoming fight in Antwerp and how I was fighting an opponent from the States and the fight was one of the few which would be televised.

"That was really good," Nina expressed as our plates were cleared away.

"You honestly can't go wrong with this place. This was my mom's little escape. She would scrape up some money when she could and bring me and my sister. We'd have to share a dish because she couldn't afford for all three of us to order something different but it didn't matter, we had each other," I explained as I thought back to those days when everything was dark, but when mom would take us out, we got a sneak peek at the light.

"Yeah, my parents struggled for a few years. I remember being made fun of in school for my hand me down clothes that were sometimes ill-fitting, but eventually Dad picked up better routes and even took on an occasional second job. We were able to get out of poverty and have a little something. Now my parents are comfortable. Dad still drives the taxi but Mom has stopped cleaning houses." It always caught me off guard that Nina didn't look like she'd been through so much, but she had.

I handed the waiter some cash to pay our bill and rose from my seat. I grabbed Nina's coat and helped her into it before she grabbed her bag. I'd loosened by bow tie by now and the links on my cuff. Dressing up wasn't really my thing.

We stepped outside where the crowds had thinned and only a few people hung around snapping a few photos and taking in the sights. Nina paused as we stood in front of City Hall together.

"What are you thinking about?" I asked, sneaking my arm back around her shoulders.

Nina peered up at me, biting her lip anxiously. My other hand cupped her cheek, her skin warm under my touch even in the cool air. I stroked her flesh with my thumb.

"I'm thinking I had a nice time. Thanks a lot, for everything. I don't normally open up to anyone really. It's never been easy. Nobody understands me," she confessed.

"I understand you," I asserted as I continued stroking her cheek and she leaned into my touch and hummed softly, her lips looking more kissable with each moment, but I was scared to go in for the kill. "Nina?"

"Hmm?"

"Can I kiss you?" The words came out and I couldn't take them back, but I didn't want to. I'd wanted to kiss her since that first night walking her home.

"Oui," her voice was almost as quiet as a mouse.

I didn't take my chances for her to take it back. I dove in and claimed her lips as my own. They were just as perfect as I imagined they would be against mine. They were soft, welcoming, and warm. The arm I had on her shoulders before was now looped around her waist and she leaned into me deeper as I intensified our kiss.

My tongue licked against her lips, causing them to part for me. Eagerly, I introduced my tongue into her mouth, finding hers as they fought this impassioned battle. Fuck, it was better than my dreams and I wasn't going to let her disappear on me again. I had to have Nina in my life one way or another and I'd prefer her this way—in my arms, mine.

Pulling away, I glanced down at her, she fought to catch her breath after our kiss before she peered up, her eyes meeting mine and a smile coming to her lips as we both noticed her hands were fisting at my shirt for dear life.

"Wow," she breathed. "I have no words."

"Me either," I confessed as I took her hand, our fingers laced together easily.

We didn't say anything else as we began toward Central Station, the place where we'd first met. I'd never had much affinity for the old train station before but now I saw it in a whole new light. It brought her into my life.

CHAPTER SIX

NINA

It was all too easy to fall for Marc in a way I'd never fallen for anyone. When I married, I was a virgin and I'd only kissed one other boy in my life when I was a teenager. Marc and all he was barged into my life and broken down every wall, fence, and barrier I had, and there was no turning back from it. The man was an addiction in every single sense.

"What do you think?" I asked Ayo who sat on my bed watching me try on every single dress I owned.

Tonight, was Marc's big fight in Antwerp and he'd given me two tickets when I'd seen him a few days ago. I didn't think we had a definition of what we were, but whatever it was, it was nice. I went by the gym when I had a free moment, and Marc would come by wherever I was performing to take me home every night. We talked about anything and everything easily and I couldn't get enough of his kisses.

"C'est très sexy," Ayo proclaimed as he stood and began to alter my dress a little bit.

"Not too sexy, right?" I asked concerned as I peered into the mirror at the red dress I wore with my braids hanging down my back.

"It's perfect. I promise. It is sexy but not doing too much. You look beautiful and I know Marc will think so too," Ayo honestly critiqued before he bumped me from in front of the mirror and began to check himself out. I rolled my eyes and picked up my purse from the bed.

"So, when are you going to tell auntie and uncle about your new beau?" Ayo questioned.

"How about never," I shrugged. My parents already felt a certain way about me since my divorce and now I was fornicating with a white man. They might as well disown me now. Ayo laughed loudly at my response. "Plus, Marc and me? I don't really know what we are."

"He's your boyfriend, bitch," Ayo pointed out matter-of-factly. "You spend every moment you can together and you're constantly making out. You two are dating, simple as that. Next. Now, let's get to this fight. I'm excited to meet your boo and check out sweaty men."

The second ticket I got could only ever go to Ayo. I wouldn't take anyone else.

———

THE LOTTO ARENA was packed from wall to wall with people eager to see the fights taking place that night. Ayo and I weaved past already drunk men and girls in bikinis pedaling beer and energy drinks. The aroma of waffles and fries wafted through the air as was typical for any event.

"Is that him?" Ayo asked in awe as he stopped in his tracks. A large banner hung from the ceiling with a photo of a man adorning it. Tall, bald, shirtless, and covered in tattoos was Marc with his arms folded, a tough scowl, and confident smirk on his lips.

HOME OF THE BELGIAN BEAST

Butterflies fluttered in my stomach at just a banner of him and I hadn't even seen him in person just yet. It was weird knowing this guy was possibly my boyfriend and according to Ayo it was definite.

"Yeah, that's Marc," I gushed before Ayo was pulling me away in the direction of our section at the sound of an announcement coming from inside. It would be starting soon, and my hands were beginning to sweat with nervous excitement.

We arrived at the door to our seating section where an attendant checked our tickets and insisted on escorting us to our seats. I understood the reason behind the escort as we arrived in the front row. I swallowed hard as we took our seats.

"Holy shit!" Ayo's hands were over his mouth as we

looked around in awe of having the best seats in the house.

A moment later, I was tapped on the shoulder and I glanced to see a wheelchair had pulled up next to my seat. It was Marc's friend, and former fighter, Fabumi who gave me a huge grin.

"It's nice to see you again," he greeted me over the loud music.

"You too. Have you seen Marc?" I asked wondering how Marc was fairing before the big fight. He'd sent me an text when he arrived in Antwerp early this morning that he couldn't wait to see me after.

"Oui, I was just with him while he warmed up. This fight is a big deal with the TV cameras," Fabumi expressed. I knew it meant a lot to Marc. He talked about it a lot as time led up to the day.

"I'm excited for him," I gushed in excitement.

Suddenly, the lights went down and the crowd came alive. Everyone around was cheering at the top of their lungs. Before the announcer could even say much of anything the arena broke out into an arousing chant of, *"Bel-gian Beast! Bel-gian Beast! Bel-gian Beast!"*

It was electric as the chant grew louder and more rousing. Everyone was on their feet and cheering at the top of their lungs; all for the one man who captured me in a way no one else could.

"Good evening, Antwerp!" The announcer cheered.

"Oh, my goodness, this is too exciting," Ayo said in my ear. I nodded enthusiastically.

Marc and I were both performers in very

different areas. I was used to a room so silent one could hear a pin drop with occasional applause filling an opera hall or theater when prompted. Marc's stage was very different with roars of applause and chants spontaneously filling a giant area.

I bent to Fabumi who clapped along with everyone else and was filled with the thrilling excitement that flooded through everyone.

"I see why he loves it so much," I told him.

"It's addicting. Being in that cage and hearing that roar. It's everything a fighter wants and needs," Fabumi expressed.

The night started with women fighters who were the fiercest competitors I'd ever seen. These women trained extremely hard for a night like this one and went into it with everything, ready to prove themselves. The crowd urged them on until one was victorious.

As the men began, the violence was kicked into high gear. I understood the sport and that they were trained for this, but from the first sight of blood, my stomach turned queasy. It was hard to watch, and I turned away often. The sound of their fists connecting with flesh brought back memories I worked hard to lock away.

"Are you okay?" Ayo asked as a fight ended with a fighter being carried out on a stretcher by paramedics and blood leaking from his face as they passed us by. I tried to swallow down the bile trying to force its way up my throat. I only nodded in response, afraid if I spoke, I'd vomit.

"Here's some water for her," a voice said from behind us. Fabumi's wife had arrived late, just after the women fought. She was a sweet girl, with almond tanned skin, and wild, dark cocoa curls. Her belly was like a round watermelon as she and Fabumi were expecting a baby in the coming weeks.

"Thanks, Emmy," Fabumi handed me a cup of water.

I took a few sips which helped calm my stomach, but the dizziness I had still remained.

"My first fights weren't easy to watch either and it doesn't help being so close," Emmy noted as Ayo rubbed my shoulder.

The arena seemed to take on a different atmosphere as the last fight of the night drew near. The music grew louder and the crowd more enthusiastic and eager for what was to come. As the octagon was cleared the announcer returned.

"Are you ready for the Belgian Beast!" His voice rumbled throughout the entire area, my stomach tying in knots thinking about Marc being in that cage and fighting with the vigor the men before him fought with. "Get ready Belgium for your home champion, the undefeated Belgian Beast himself, Marc Vandenberghe versus the Bull of the U.S.A., Colin Smith!"

The chants began again, the thumping of my heart pounding harder and faster with each chant of, *"Belgian Beast!"*

Suddenly, the chorus turned into uncontrollable screams as Marc emerged with a spotlight on him. His stature alone commanded the room like nothing I'd ever witnessed. His pure power on display as he began to walk toward the caged octagon. He passed us; his eyes met mine for a brief second before he continued on his way with Jean following not far behind him.

Fabumi, Emmy, and Ayo were all going completely nuts as Marc took to the octagon with power the prestige. I stood in complete silence, afraid of what the outcome would be for either side. I swallowed hard.

"Allez Marc!" Fabumi shouted from his chair.

My heart thumped so loudly in my ears it almost blocked out the ongoing and enthusiastic chants of everyone in the arena.

Marc's opponent came out to mostly boos from the crowd who were all there to see the country's hero defend his championship and keep his undefeated title.

At the sound of the bell, the opponent from the US took a swing Marc dodged easily. I followed Marc's every move through the cage. He was like a skilled dancer as he moved in reaction to the other man locked in with him.

They were all over one another so quick, I almost missed it. Marc had Colin to the ground and was laying into him. At the first splatter of blood, I lost the contents of my stomach into the cup. I couldn't take it.

I jolted to my feet and jogged toward the exit, and out into the nearly empty hall as everyone was inside glued to the fight. I stood against a wall and bent down to steady myself. Only a moment later, a hand was on my back rubbing it. It was Ayo. I wanted to support Marc, but it was too much to see him in that light, watching him beat the living shit out of a man. I'd seen it once before and I didn't want to see it again.

"And your winner is your champion, Marc Vandenberghe, the Belgian Beast!" The announcer cheered to the eruption of everyone. The vibrations of everyone shook the floor under our feet.

"It's over," Ayo told me, and I nodded. I was glad it was over.

———

WE ALL STOOD WAITING for the man of the evening to make his appearance. When the fight ended, I was able to gather myself and return to my seat to watch Marc receive his belt. He beamed proudly at his accomplishments and he should be proud of how hard he worked to achieve it.

The door to the locker room opened into the hall and Jean emerged first with a huge grin on his face before Marc followed him proudly. With his chest out, he stepped out the door with his belt over his shoulder.

Fabumi was first to congratulate him with Emmy before he stepped to me. I felt everyone's eyes on us as he approached me and slipped an arm around my waist. In his arms, I had this safety net that calmed everything down around me and locked me into him.

"Ma petite danseuse," he muttered down to me as he pulled me in close.

I inhaled his freshly showered scent.

"I'm happy you came."

"I'm happy you won," I noted before Ayo cleared his throat clearly craving some attention from the star of the night. I shook my head before I turned toward my cousin who was eager to meet Marc. "Marc, meet my cousin, Ayo."

"Enchanté." Marc said as he extended his free hand to Ayo who shook it. "I don't know about everybody else but I'm starving. Jean made us reservations at the Spanish place around the corner. Sound good?"

"Perfect," I said up to Marc who refused to let me go.

As we started toward the exit, Marc and I ended up toward the back of the pack. Fabumi lead the way with Jean as Emmy and Ayo enthusiastically chatted. Taking a moment, Marc took a pause and bent to me, he kissed me gently but as I'd learned with Marc, gentle never lasted long. His lips claimed mine fiercely, before my body was pressed into a wall out of the sight of everyone else. We were alone for a moment and captured in one another.

"I heard you got sick?" Marc questioned as he pulled away.

I nodded, partly ashamed I couldn't stomach sitting through the fight.

"You don't have to come to my fights. I understand

it is not for everyone to watch. It's fucking intense," Marc noted to my enthusiastic nodding on response.

"A little much for me."

"It's okay." Marc bent, kissing me again, taking my breath away.

"What are we?" I blurted out as soon as he pulled away. "Do you see me as your girlfriend?"

"Fuck yes. I wouldn't see it any other way." He leaned over me and cupped my cheek stroking it with his thumb. It resolved and complicated things in a way. He wasn't exactly who my family would ever see me with, and I vowed to myself to keep us a secret when it came to them.

"That clears things up, I suppose," I joked as I stood expertly on the tips of my toes and pressed my lips to his.

I allowed him to press his body onto mine as I absorbed his body heat. With a hand on the wall, his other one pulled my up my leg around his waist while his lips travelled down to my neck and rained kisses over my collarbone. I caught myself moaning at the stimulating kisses. We'd never gone further than kisses, and as much as I wanted more, I was afraid of the can of worms it could open. There was no going back for me once I gifted my body to him.

"Where'd they go?" Fabumi's voice echoed from around the corner.

"Où êtes vous?" Ayo called for us.

Playfully, I pressed my hand against Marc's chest

and slipped from under him before I began to stroll in the direction of the others.

"Where are you going?" Marc stood back, having not taken a step, his arms crossed over his chest, his hard-worked muscles bulging.

"I'm going to eat. Are you coming?" I smirked back in his direction only to pull a smile from him.

He dashed in my direction and pulled me into his arms from behind. I squealed loudly as he pressed his lips to my neck and pulled me in tight.

"Found them," Ayo pointed out as he came around the corner with a sly look on his face. "Come on love birds, we want to eat."

Love, what exactly did that feel like? Was it the butterflies I had whenever Marc looked my way, the sense of security I felt when he was near, or the overwhelming emotions that filled my entire body just from just the thought of him? Could it be all of that wrapped into one complicated and vast emotion? I was eager and afraid to eventually find out.

"THANK YOU FOR COMING," Marc murmured down to me as we stood at my front door. He stood over me with an arm around me and the butterflies in my stomach dancing away as usual. "I'm sorry it was a little much for you."

"It's okay. I'm glad I could support you," I told him

as I shivered in the cold. "Do you want to come inside? Its cold."

"Yeah, let's get in."

I unlocked my door and Marc followed me in as he usually did when he came home with me on some of the evenings he traveled home with me from my performances. Entering my apartment, I was quick to kick off the heels I'd been in all night. Marc dropped his bag near the door and settled on the couch.

"Venez ici," Marc beckoned me over with a finger.

I obliged.

His arms pulled me into his lap and I naturally cuddled into his arms.

Everything with Marc felt natural from the flutter in my tummy to his arms holding me close. I relished in how natural it felt to be with him. I'd never felt safer or more cared for. Marc shared this level of dedication to me I'd never felt with anyone. I'd never had anything like it before and I craved moments like this, but they also scared me so intensely that my heart thumped with anxiety. Behind it all, I had a fear of it disappearing on me and turning into smoke.

"How old were you when you got married?" Marc twirled the end of one of my braids between his fingers.

"Twenty-one. I'd just been offered my first job dancing and I turned it down. I regretted that moment every single day. I spent three years trapped and afraid of what could happen if I finally decided to leave. I found out when enough was enough. When I lost my baby..." My voice trailed off and Marc quickly wiped away the tears that were falling from my eyes.

At the time I was already living in a nightmare. Every single day I never knew the man that would step into my front door. Would he be caring or a living nightmare?

He'd finally managed to get me pregnant after nearly three years of telling me that something must be wrong with me and that I was broken. That pregnancy didn't last long. I'd said something out of turn one evening and he as usual made sure I paid for it, but that night was the worst beating I'd received including being shoved down a flight of stairs in his drunken rage.

"I swear monsters like that shouldn't be allowed to walk this earth. I'm glad you got out before you could have children and before those children could watch the horrors he unleashed on you. Having been a witness, I can tell you the scars last forever. I hear my father's voice every single time I fight. It fuels me in a strange way," Marc expressed as he continued to play around with my braids.

"It's the same for me but I try to not hear my ex-husband's voice. Just the thought of his voice makes my skin crawl and I can't breathe. It was so hard coming out of that. I'm grateful for the medications my doctor provided me with to help my worsened depression and tipping anxiety." I looked into Marc's eyes as they watched me, blue and piercing.

Not wanting to talk about it anymore, I puckered

my lips and kissed him. I caught myself smiling with my mouth still against his. I pulled away but stared at him for another moment.

"Its like you came out of nowhere and fell easily into my life," I was still astonished at our story.

Marc kissed me gently before he pulled away this time.

"Nothing is chance," Marc whispered his lips brushing over mine. "There's always a purpose."

CHAPTER SEVEN

MARC

With my lips to her shoulder, I rained kisses across her bare skin in hopes of waking her up. Slowly Nina began to stir from her peaceful slumber. We'd gone to bed as the sun began to rise after spending a couple of hours just talking, and kissing. Nina held this purity about her that I respected and even though we slept in the same bed, it was only sleeping and nothing more. Going any further would be up to Nina as much as I ached to pin her under me and make sweet love to her.

"Bonjour," she whispered through her sleepy haze before I captured her plump lips with my own.

It was hard to keep calm while I had her in bed and her plump ass resting against my cock. I knew she felt my hard on easily but was lady like and ignored it while she kissed me back.

"Do you want to come with me today?" I asked as I sat up. I had to or I'd go too far with her. It was too easy to when I was in bed with the sexiest woman I'd ever met. Her sensuality was more eluded when put out there obviously. She didn't have to flaunt her body to turn me on. From the way she looked at me through her long eyelashes to the firm plumpness of her lips made me want her.

"I can. Let me take a shower," she answered before she yawned, her hands going over her mouth instinctively.

"Okay," I murmured as I took in her bedroom. It was my first time inside of it.

The small apartment's single bedroom was painted in a soft daisy yellow color. The walls had framed pieces of artwork all featuring dancers. Next to the mirror though were a bunch of personal photos tacked to the wall like a scrapbook.

I stood from the bed and stretched before I strolled to where Nina's photos hung. There was one I recognized right away as her as a small girl with afro puff ponytails and a missing toothed grin.

"Très mignon," I commented to the woman who pulled the duvet to her face in embarrassment.

There was a candid photo of a teenaged Nina with a younger boy I knew right away was her hilarious cousin, Ayo. They were more best friends than cousins and he was the only family member she had to count on with her deepest secrets and thoughts when it came to the world around her. Nina obviously loved her parents, but she couldn't talk to them openly from what she'd told me. She constantly had a fear of their judgment.

"I'm going to let you shower. I'm going home to do the same. I'll see you soon?" I questioned to Nina who nodded as I trekked back in her direction.

With a finger under her chin, I pulled her face up and bent to give her a chaste kiss. It never got old, kissing her. Each time was just as exciting as the last. I'd immediately wanted her to be mine and now she was.

Hungry for more, I crushed my mouth into hers and climbed onto the bed, my body pressed hers to the mattress as our tongues fought an impassioned battle. My hand slipped under the hem of the tank top she wore to bed and my fingertips crushed over her supple skin.

Like a bucket of ice water, the reality of going further hit me. I wanted her more than anything, but it was up to Nina when and how it happened. She was in the driver's seat and I'd handed over the keys. It was so unlike me, but she was changing me.

"I'll go. See you in thirty minutes," I said down to her as I stood back up.

"Thirty minutes," she managed to breathe before she lifted her body up. "Thank you for going slow with me." She stood on her toes left a brisk and easy kiss on my lips. It was as if she knew my very thoughts.

"It's all up to you, baby," I told her honestly. I wanted Nina to always have complete trust in me and how I'd treat her. She was important to me and not just somebody to warm my bed. I knew fairly quickly I wanted Nina around for the long haul if she'd have me.

NINA'S ARMS were wrapped tightly around my waist as we rode off through Brussels on my motorbike. Across the city on a sleepy Sunday, we arrived on a narrow street in Kraainem. The connected brick houses all stood in a row and we parked in front of one with colorful flower boxes on the windowsill. The last blooms before the frigid and drying winter arrived.

I collected Nina's helmet and secured it to the bike with my own before I took her with me by the waist and we stepped to the front door. I rang the doorbell and was greeted by the sound of my mother's voice.

"Wie is het?" She questioned from the other side of the door in her thick and unmistakable Flemish accent.

"Jouw zoon," I answered before the door swung open and there stood the woman who didn't just carry me for nine months, and birth me, but did everything in her power to protect me even when she couldn't.

She didn't quite look like the young woman she was when I was a little boy, but she was still just as beautiful even with age. Though she had wrinkles here and there, she kept her hair blonde and her smile was always just as bright when she saw me now as when I'd run out of the school gates to her at the end of the day.

"Marc," she beamed as she pulled me into a tight hug. Well, as tight as a short little woman like my mother could. "You have a guest." She quickly noted Nina as she pulled away.

Nina shyly smiled from behind me and I was quick to pull her forward with me, my arm firm around her petite waist.

"Maman, this is my girlfriend, Nina. Nina this is my mother," I introduced the two women switching to French. I'd learned that Nina did speak Dutch but preferred French. Mom quickly pulled Nina in for a kiss on the cheek and Nina did the same.

"Come inside, I was in the garden getting the furniture put away before the bad weather really begins," My mother explained switching to French herself as she allowed Nina and I into the house and closed the door behind us. "Nina, that is a lovely name."

"Merci," Nina answered in her soft voice as we walked toward the back of the house and just into the kitchen I could see where a man sat at a table with a freshly poured beer. "You didn't mention we'd meet your mother," Nina whispered back to me as we continued to follow my mother.

"Surprise," I shrugged playfully to Nina who shook her head at me as we continued to follow along.

"Luc, Marc is here with his girlfriend!" My mother called up the hall.

After my father, my mom spent time healing from her wounds and during that time she met Luc. He was an insurance agent she met while applying for one of her first jobs since being a housewife and now being the sole breadwinner of the house. They meshed perfectly with one another and for the first time my mother was in a healthy relationship.

"There's the big man!" Luc's voice boomed as he stood and pulled me into a hug and patted me enthusiastically on the back. "I watched the fight on TV last night, great job."

"Thank you."

"Luc watched, I went to bed," Mom told us. "I can't take watching those fights," she told Nina.

"Nina didn't do too well there. It was a little much for her," I pulled out a chair for her to sit before I sat down next to her.

"I can't do all that violence. It's too much for me but Marc makes his living doing it and he takes care of my poor Sophie." Mom sighed as she mentioned my sister who no one wanted to think of as a lost cause, but it never seemed to get better. "She came by with the kids last night. She and Basir had gotten into an argument."

"I don't know what else to do, Maman," I confessed.

"She'll have to figure it out on her own, but I hope she can do it quickly for the sake of the children and poor Basir. He's a good man and works so many jobs to keep the children clothed and fed only for Sophie to gamble it all away sometimes." Mom shook her head as she pulled a couple beers from the fridge.

"Want a drink?" she questioned.

"None for me. I'm driving and it's Friday so…" My voice trailed off not knowing if Nina would want a drink.

"That's right, day of prayer and all, I better not, but

thank you," Nina said politely.

"You're Muslim?" My stepfather asked intrigued with an eyebrow raised. I already felt him casting a judgmental eye upon her. I sat up a little straighter and glared in his direction as I awaited Nina's answer and his subsequent response.

"I am," Nina answered meekly. I could sense that she was uncomfortable discussing it. She tended to not speak about her religion much at all and I respected that as everyone else should.

"Where is your family from?" My mom asked also intrigued to know more about Nina.

"They migrated from Mali right before I was born," Nina expertly explained as I held her hand and stroked my thumb over the back of her hand in reassurance.

"That's lovely," my mom said happily as she peered at Luc, clearly giving him a look to keep him in check.

Luc was a good guy and loved my mom, but he could be xenophobic. He'd been known to stir up drama with Basir on occasion in regard to Basir's Moroccan origins and Islamic faith.

"It was a good fight. The American put up a fuss. I kept waiting for him to go down and stay down," Luc expressed as he went back to the subject of last night's match. "When he took that last stumble, I knew that was it for him."

"Oui, he was a good opponent. It gets boring when I take them down quick," I conversed as my mom and Luc sipped their beers. Mom cringed at talks of my fights.

"No more talk of those fights. I'm glad you won but please," My mother begged. I gave her a sympathetic nod. "How long have you two been together? Marc never brings girls around."

"Mom!" I quipped. I knew the questions would come and that she was itching to get as much information as she could from Nina and myself.

My mother huffed in mock frustration.

"I just want a little information. I can't remember the last time you brought a girl home. I know there have been girls in your life, but you never bring them home which means Nina is one special lady." My mom beamed as she peered over to Nina who nervously played with my hand that laid in her lap.

"That she is," I confirmed before I leaned over and kissed Nina on the cheek.

"Ik ben gelukkig," Mom cheered as she expressed her happiness. "I only want you to be happy, Marc. You've sacrificed so much for our family. It's time you enjoy your happiness. Maybe even give up fighting and settle down. I want you safe and happy."

"If I can promise anything, it is that I'll be happy," I confirmed.

Giving up fighting wasn't in the cards yet. One day I'd step out of the octagon for the last time, but it just wasn't time yet. I still had so much to prove, and I still felt the fight raging through my veins, pulsating with energy.

———

WITH MY FISTS pummeling into the bag. I proved to myself why I was called the Belgian Beast. With each jab at the leather bag, I saw myself in the octagon against an opponent fighting them with everything in me. In my fantasy, I was showing the world who the beast really was. I knew who I was but did everyone else see it?

"Come on, Marc," Jean cheered from next to me. He was egging me on and forcing me to go harder, which was his job. He molded me from an angry boy into a legitimate fighter.

The endorphins rushing through my veins made me feel invincible. My skin felt as if it was in flames as I stayed in my zone. Grunting with each punch and kicking high as if I was going directly into an opponent's neck.

As Jean called time, I growled into the air. I worked hard from the gym to the cage. This wasn't just for show, I put in every fucking moment of blood, sweat, and tears. With a splash of water to my face, I finally refocused on the room around me. The gym was empty except for Jean and I as most intense sessions were.

"Good practice," Jean noted with a slap on my sweat covered back. I could only manage a grunt in response before chucking down an entire bottle of water. "We've got to keep this up for your next big one. New York is going to be an entirely different monster than we've ever dealt with before and I need your focus as high as you can get it."

"Done," I declared simply before I sat down on the

edge of the beat-up leather couch, not far from my usual practice area.

"I'm serious, Marc. No distractions and practice, practice, practice."

"I said, done," I growled, frustrated at Jean's pushing. I knew what I had to do, and I did it every single time.

"I'm sorry but that girl has become a distraction and I know you care about her but—."

"Nothing," I cut him off with a bark as I stood to my feet, my stance towering over the short man. "Nina isn't a distraction. She doesn't stop me from doing what needs to be done."

"Just making sure, that's all." Jean raised in hands on defeat. "I can tell she means a lot to you. She's a nice girl and you do need a nice girl, but the key is to not let the nice girl get in the way of the prize."

"She is the prize," I admitted openly. "I've never felt like this about any girl I've had anything with and yes, most girls were just drive by flings."

"Is the Belgian Beast in love?" Jean asked with a light chuckle.

Love, that was the biggest little word I could think of. There was so much wrapped into that one word that I didn't know where to begin. I didn't know what love was and now I had this woman in my life who changed the game in only moments. Was that love? I had no clue but was more than prepared to find out with her and her only.

"He's definitely in love," Fabumi's voice broke my concentration.

My head snapped up to see him rolling in from the old elevator shaft. The elevator hadn't ever worked but as soon as Fabumi had his accident, Jean made sure it was functioning again just for him.

Jean had a son who tragically passed away at the age of five from leukemia. He and his wife divorced after their son's death and he threw himself into his career as a fighting coach. His athletes became his children and he took Fabumi and I under his wing as his sons when we needed it the most.

"Mon frère," I greeted my friend as he wheeled over to my training area. "And I wouldn't call it love. I've barely known her a month, but I do know it's different."

"It's love. Don't fight it, man. I agree, she's nice. A little quiet and on the reserved side but nice. There is a little something about her, a spark. You can sense it and I think that's what brings you two together," Fabumi reflected.

"What are you, some expert on the matter?" I joked playfully with my best friend.

Fabumi chuckled and shrugged. "Hell, maybe. I'm just a ball of love lately anyway. I'm about to be a dad and all. I don't know if I'm an expert, but I do know life is too short to not go after what you want. If you want her, go for it. I think she wants you too."

I think she does too.

CHAPTER EIGHT

NINA

I settled into complete security as I leaned into Marc's arms while we stood in line at the neighborhood friterie. It was a long night for me with another intense performance with our prima ballerina out once again and myself filling in for her. Though tired, I was grateful I could prove myself as a dancer worthy of commanding the stage.

When I returned to dance, I had something to prove immediately, I'd turned down a job in Paris before I got married. My career in ballet had shot off right away but the pause had given me a sort of reputation, at least I felt it had. Returning to dance, I wanted to show I still had it and could be a prima.

Marc ordered for the two of us. I stayed firmly wrapped in his arms during the busy Saturday night rush of everyone who didn't want to cook dinner and would partake in Belgium's fast food staple, fries.

As what had become our usual, Marc had come to

meet me at the backdoor of the Opera House, and we took the train to Jette as we'd done the night we met. From that very night, I couldn't quite put my finger on exactly what there was about me that kept him close. I saw myself as frankly forgetful, but Marc didn't forget, he made it a mission to know me for more than the ballerina he stumbled upon. I didn't know why when there were plenty of women out there for him, but he picked me.

"Merde, c'est the Belgian Beast!" An excited voice wailed from the seating area of the shop. A man shot out of his seat and stumbled over a chair before he arrived at Marc and me.

I could smell the alcohol leaking through his pores as he stepped a little too close. I cringed at the smell of him. It was so close to nights when my ex-husband would come home drunk out of his mind with the alcohol seeping out of him and the stench filling our home.

Marc must have felt me flinch as he rubbed a hand over my arm gently and gave me a kiss on the forehead before he stepped alone to the eagerly enthusiastic fan.

"Bonsoir," Marc said easily in his deep and relaxing voice. "Ça va?" He politely asked as he reached out and shook the man's hand.

"Merde, merde, merde!" He chanted over and over clearly in shock that Marc even spoke to him. "Ça va. I'm a big fan. Can I get a picture?" The man yanked his phone from his pocket and poked around at it as he tried his best to open his camera app.

Taking a selfie with his fan, Marc was completely relaxed. I had no idea how he did it. Watching him, my heart raced and there was a hard lump in my throat. If I had to deal with any type of admirer, I wouldn't be able to handle it for one moment with my anxiety getting the best of me. Marc was so different, he made everything look so easy. I was in jealous awe as I watched him casually converse with the man who was glued to his every word.

Marc was somewhat of a homegrown idol. It wasn't the first time I'd been out with him and someone spotted him and went into a flurry of excitement. Each time, I respectfully stood to the side while Marc interacted.

"Merci, merci, merci," the man slurred repeatedly as he stumbled back to his seat with his group of friends.

Marc returned to me as our order was placed on the counter. Marc paid, and we were easily off with a wave to his fan before we stepped outside and began the walk toward Marc's apartment.

"You're Mr. Popular," I joked as I peered up at Marc who simply gave me a wink. "I don't know how you do it. You're so easygoing. I wouldn't be able to speak, let alone have a casual conversation with someone who recognized me on the street."

"It's not too hard. In a weird way, I know these people already. They love what I love," Marc explained as we strolled together, my fingers laced with his and the butterflies going insane in my stomach. "It used to be harder. I don't know. I've changed so much since

I've met you. I mean I've always been confident, but my confidence is different."

"I just don't have the nerves for it," I concluded with a shrug.

"You've got nerves of steel Ms. Nina Sangare. You gave them to me."

I laughed in response to his claim. I didn't have nerves at all. I spent much of my time over analyzing and overthinking everything. I generally scared myself out of most opportunities. Being with Marc, I'd left the house more than I'd ever done. My life generally consisted of teaching, dancing, home, and Friday's with my family.

With Marc, I was constantly somewhere with him. He was the extrovert to my introvert.

Arriving at Marc's apartment, he handed me our package of fries while he opened the doors and we took the elevator to the top floor of the four-story building. We headed directly to the living room table where Marc preferred to eat most meals.

I settled down on the black leather couch, took off my shoes before sitting cross legged as I waited for Marc who reappeared a moment later in his usual gray sweatpants hanging low around his waist, without a shirt. I swallowed as my eyes roamed over his robust arms, and intricate tattoos over his muscular chest. He stood for a moment handsome, hypnotic, powerful, and I knew he knew it. I allowed my eyes to follow the V of his lower stomach into his pants where the outline of his dick was clearly defined.

"Ready to eat?" Marc plopped down next to me. I got a whiff of his scent and I stopped breathing for a moment. Marc kept me on edge every moment I was with him and I didn't even think he was trying. It was all his natural allure I was drawn to.

"Mmmhmm," I answered innocently as I tried to force my mind away from what was waiting for me in his pants when I decided I was ready, and something tingling inside whispered that I was ready.

I leaned over to Marc with my heart pounding out of my chest and pressed my hips to his, hard. Naturally as our kiss intensified, and with my agile flexibility, I slipped my body over his straddling him with the intense need of feeling his hard body against mine.

Having no experience in initiating anything intimate wasn't even apparent as it all felt incredibly natural. Wanting every part of him didn't feel abominable or sinful. Nothing besides dance had ever felt so strangely right.

Allowing my hips to roll over his, the tips of his fingers roamed under the back of my shirt while my hands settled on his warm chest.

I pulled away to catch my breath, disappointed in breaking our moment I glanced down into Marc's iced blazing eyes.

"It's only what you want. What do you want ma petite danseuse?" Marc removed one of his hands from my hips and cupped my face.

"Je te veux."

Marc didn't need any more words before he

gripped me tightly, crushed his mouth to mine, and stood.

My legs wrapped tightly around his body as his cock pressed into my awaiting center. I ground my hips onto him as he briskly moved us from the living room, and down a short hall. A dim light flipped on, and I broke away to find us in a large bedroom. It wasn't the small musty bedroom I'd expected but a sophisticated bachelor space. The walls were all a dark shade of crimson, the bed had a black leather headboard, and a dark gray duvet with pillows. Over the headboard, a Belgian flag was framed.

Gently, Marc laid me on the bed and his fingers got started unbuttoning my jeans before he stripped them easily down my legs, and his hands settled on my thighs. His eyes pierced me intensely and with a devotion I'd never seen in the eyes of anyone else. It was me he wanted, and I found it difficult to grasp why.

"You know," he began. "You're perfect to me."

I didn't know what to say in response. I didn't see myself as perfect to anyone, not even my own family.

Marc quickly stripped me from my panties before taking my hands and pulling me into a seated position. I acted before he could and pulled my shirt over my head, exposing my bare breasts to him. My nipples perked at the cold air and Marc grinned down at my naked body.

"Give me one second, ma petite danseuse," he disappeared out a door. I saw a light flip on for a moment before hearing what sounded like cabinets before he returned with a small package in his hand, a condom.

At the sight of the condom, it struck me that this was real. I was giving myself to him in a way I'd never done before. Sex with my ex-husband was never romantic and more done out of duty. I hated it and for the first time it was something I wanted to give and enjoy as I'd heard it was meant to be.

Marc set the condom on the bed next to me before his hands settled back on my thighs caressing them as his hands slid down my knees before spreading my legs. I couldn't help but moan in pure anticipation as Marc's hands found themselves on the band of his sweatpants. He began to drag them down at a lazy pace, my eyes following from his stomach and down into the dark hairs that began to appear.

My eyes gawked as his dick came into view. It was as girthy as I'd imagined with his bulging body. My inexperience made me feel inadequate, but my raging hormones couldn't care less. My body needed his.

Marc stood before me, his hand stroking his erection as his eyes met mine.

"You want this. Tell me how bad," Marc demanded in a gruff voice that sent a shiver down my spine through my core.

This was nothing like the sex I'd experienced before, and it was already so much more exciting and inclusive. Marc wanted my input. I had a voice in this.

"Are you going to tell me?" He took a step closer to the bed.

My legs twisted together, and I bit down on my bottom lip.

"Fuck. You look so fucking sexy like that. Please tell me, baby."

He stepped closer and settled his hands on my knees before spreading my legs apart. I swallowed hard before a bravery I only felt when going on stage took over.

"Marc, I want it," I panted desperately to his satisfied smile.

He bent to me, his lips placing a kiss on my belly button.

I giggled as his ticklish kisses rained over my flat stomach, but my giggles quickly turned to moans as his kisses got lower and lower before his tongue slipped up my awaiting slit, and his fingers spread me open.

Every single sensation going through me was brand new. I'd never had a man's mouth down on me and the electricity zinging through me made me feel faint. My hands found his bald head and hung on as his tongue lapped over my overly sensitive clit.

I cried out into his bedroom, my hips riding into his mouth and fingers that had buried themselves inside me, pumping in and out.

"Marc," I gasped as my first non-self-given orgasm rolled through my core and I shook under him.

Marc arose with a satisfied smile on his lips. My chest heaved as I watched him deliriously. I didn't know what had come over me, but I desperately needed more.

"You taste so good," Marc mumbled as he licked his lips.

"I guess that's a good thing," I shyly reckoned.

Marc chuckled as he climbed onto the bed and settled between my open legs. He bent to me and kissed me gently at first, but it quickly intensified as his tongue teased my lips into parting. With my fingernails digging into his shoulders, I held onto him as he hiked up my leg and gripped my backside.

Breaking our kiss, he nibbled my bottom lip.

"I need to be inside you so fucking bad," he declared in his gruff voice as his lips brushed over mine.

"Please," I begged. "I'm ready, Marc. I want your Belgian Beast."

"Fuck, I like that. My Belgian Beast," Marc kissed me once more before he lifted up and sat back on his knees. He grabbed the condom off the bed and ripped the package open.

I watched his every move as he took the condom from its foil packaging and began to work it onto his dick. I watched, amazed at how the rubber stretched to meet his generous size.

Once finished, Marc gave me a grin before pulling his body back over mine. Anxiously, I swallowed again. I'd only ever been with one man before and this was so incredibly new to me. I didn't quite know what to expect, but I didn't want to back out now.

"Marc," I breathed as his eyes met mine.

"Oui, ma petite danseuse," he murmured before

kissing my forehead gently which already set me at ease a great deal.

"Be gentle, it has been a long time since my last."

"Don't worry. I'll take care of you."

I smiled up at him before his lips found mine again.

Marc positioned himself at my entrance and I held my breath until his thumb pressed to my clit. A jolt rushed up my core, relaxing me as he began to penetrate me slowly and with care. I gasped as I began to stretch to his size but froze once the jingle of my phone cut through our silence. I would have ignored the call completely but that specific joyful tone was reserved for when my mother called.

"I have to answer," I told Marc in an instant panic. It was late and my mother only called late if there was an emergency.

Marc quickly pulled out and off me. I already missed the feel of him but there was no time to think about it as I jumped from his bed and found my discarded jeans. Reaching into my pocket, I found my phone. My mother's photo was staring up at me and I swiped with a jittering finger.

"Maman, what's wrong?" I answered in a panic.

"It's me," my brother's voice said from the other end. "Mom is too upset to talk. Dad had a heart attack. We just got to the hospital and he's been rushed back."

"I'm coming," I cried with hot tears instantly streaming down my cheeks.

Ending the call, I turned to Marc who watched me with deep concern. I could barely speak as I was shaking intensely and tried to find the rest of my clothes.

"Nina, Nina, what's wrong?" Marc placed his hands on my shoulders and pulled me to him.

I sobbed against his chest. I was scared my dad could die and worried for my mom at the same time. They were one another's backbone in everything.

"Mon père," I sobbed.

"What's happened, love?"

"He's had a heart attack. I have to go. I have to go to the hospital. I have to go," I panicked once again as I ripped myself away from him to find my things.

"Stop, I've got you," Marc demanded as he pulled me to standing and then sat me on the bed. I watched him pick up my things from the floor and handed them to me easily, one by one.

"Merci, merci," I sniffed as I tried to control my hysterical tears.

"We'll get dressed and I'll take you to the hospital, okay?"

"Okay."

MY HEART POUNDED out of my chest as Marc's motorcycle pulled up to the front doors of the hospital. Tears pricked my eyes once more as I stared at the automatic doors entering the small Catholic hospital in Halle.

I swung my leg over the bike and got off. Standing

steady, I took my helmet off as Marc removed his own. He wrapped an arm around my waist and pulled me close for a moment.

"It's going to be okay," he reminded me sweetly before giving me a chaste kiss.

I nodded before once again peering over to the doors, afraid of what I'd learn when I went inside.

Marc began to dismount the bike as well, but I stopped him with my hand on his chest.

"What's wrong?"

"Not now," I said, my voice soft as he cupped my cheek.

"Okay. If you need anything, call me. I'm here in a moment," he told me before kissing me again in an attempt to set me at ease.

I nodded as I handed him my helmet and slipped from his arms.

"Merci," I gave him a wave before turning toward the hospital and taking a deep breath.

Something about me felt dirty. Maybe it was my fault and I was being punished by Allah for giving my body so easily to this man. Marc to me wasn't just any man, I cared for him so deeply that it scared me. Yet, I was conflicted.

"You've always been a dirty whore," my ex-husband's voice pierced through my brain the moment I stepped into the hospital. *"You deserve any punishment you get."*

A tear escaped and trickled down my cheek as I turned into the emergency room waiting area where I saw my mother with her head on my brother's shoulder. She gasped at the sight of me and I sprinted toward them. We all hugged tightly and cried without words.

"Dirty whore."

I tried to swallow my shame, but it covered me from head to toe.

―――――

MY PHONE BUZZED in my pocket again. I pulled it out to see his name again, and again I ignored the call and put my phone right back in my pocket as I sat on the hard plastic chair of my dad's hospital room. I glanced over to Dad who was fast asleep and hooked up to so many machines it was insanity.

"He's worried about you. Maybe you should answer one of his calls," Ayo leaned over to me.

Ayo had been my constant companion at the hospital the last few days as we all took turns staying with Dad who'd had a triple bypass surgery after the major heart attack which nearly killed him.

"No, I can't," I insisted as I never allowed my eyes to leave Dad, who breathed slowly.

"Why? He just wants to make sure you're okay. It's not that hard to answer your boyfriend's call. He cares about you and I know you care about him. Hell, I think you love him," Ayo reasoned to me shaking my head.

"Stop. I don't love him," asserted as I turned to my cousin, my eyes blazing. "I need to let it go. This is all my fault." I nodded over to my dad.

"That your dad has a heart attack?" Ayo questioned. "That's not your fault, that's nature. That's your dad being allergic to exercise and constantly eating greasy foods. You've got nothing to do with that."

"Marc and I were having sex," I whispered as if dad was listening in. "I'm being punished. I know I am."

Ayo shook his head and took my hand into his and squeezed it tight.

"Listen to me, you aren't being punished for being in love or even having sex. Believe me, if it were the case, I'd be burning in the flames right this moment. Stop sabotaging what you have going for you. Your life is good right now," Ayo reasoned as he normally did. He was constantly the voice of reason when it came to everything going on in my head. "And I think Marc loves you too."

My heart skipped beats and my butterflies danced, but I was still afraid. My family would judge me, and I didn't know if I could come back again. I glanced at Dad. He put so much faith in me and I never wanted to let him down. My divorce was a blow to him, and I felt ashamed every single time I was around him because of it. The day I got married was such a proud day for him and then I ended it. I wasn't sure if he'd ever be that proud of me for something I truly wanted.

I knew I had to let this idea of being the perfect daughter go, but with my perfectionist ways, it was harder than it should be. I could give all those ideas away for Marc's love, but I could lose my family in the process.

CHAPTER NINE

MARC

As the sliding doors of the hospital opened, I stepped through and glanced around, not sure where to go. It'd been days since I'd spoken to Nina who continued to ignore my calls. Luckily, Ayo and Emmy had struck up a friendship and I learned from her Nina was practically living at the hospital.

Stepping to an information desk, I knew the only way to find Nina was to find her dad. Hell, if I had to stalk every floor of the hospital, I would.

"Hallo, can I help you?" The older woman at the counter asked me in Dutch.

"Ja," I answered. "I need the room of Mohamed Sangare?"

The woman typed into her computer and clicked around before she nodded and wrote something down on a Post-It note before handing it to me.

I read the number written on the paper, *417*.

"Dank u wel," I thanked her before I jogged off to the closest elevator anxious to see Nina after so long.

Our night together was so easy. The feel of her bare body under mine was something I could never forget. That connection forged through our intimate contact was so fucking intense it took everything in me to force myself to allow her to walk away even if she had to. Since then, she wasn't returning my calls.

I took the elevator to the fourth floor and glanced around to find the room. Counting down, I reached room four-hundred seventeen. I saw her sitting on a chair with Ayo by her side and two other women in the room. One of them I could tell right away was her mother whom Nina favored.

For the first time, I was fucking nervous. I wasn't one to get nervous, but my hands were sweating, and my heart was palpitating quickly.

Nina's mother held a cup and leaned over the hospital bed where a large frail man drank from it through a straw.

With a deep breath, I knocked on the frame of the door. Nina's head shot up and her eyes widened at the sight of me. I gave her a soft smile and a wave, but Nina didn't return the same gesture. Her eyes looked panicked as she jumped to her feet and rushed in my direction.

Arriving to me, she shut the door behind her and pulled me up the hall toward the lobby of the floor. Once far enough away from the room she turned toward me with ferocity burning in her eyes.

"What are you doing here?" She snapped anxiously as she glanced around to make sure she wasn't followed.

"I came to check on you. You haven't been answering my calls or text messages. I was worried, baby," I took her hand into mine and caressed the back with my thumb.

"You can't be here," she shot as she snatched her hand from mine. "Please leave."

"Why?" I asked realizing how she kept looking around to see if anyone was watching us. It hit me. She didn't want her family knowing about me at all. I was a secret. "You don't want your family to know you're seeing someone? But it's not just that, right?" I saw her eyes shift and I connected the dots. "You don't want them to know you're with a white man? Is that right?"

"That's not it," she insisted but I knew that wasn't true at all. Nina was hiding our relationship there was no doubt about that, but she lied to me.

"Don't fucking lie to me," I hissed angrily. Lying was one of those things I hated with everything in me and I despised it. Being honest and truthful was one of those virtues I held close. "Tell me, Nina, are you hiding us from your family?"

"Yes," she admitted in a small voice. "Please Marc, I can't do this right now. Just go. I'll call you later, I promise."

"Don't fucking expect me to answer," I fumed before I pushed past her and to the elevator that was luckily opening up.

A man whom I recognized from photos in Nina's house was getting out. It was her older brother. I watched from the elevator as he approached her.

"Ça va?"

"Ça va. I'm fine," she lied through her teeth with her eyes on me before the elevator doors closed and she disappeared from my sight.

"Fuck," I growled wanting to punch something but there was nothing to lay my fists into.

With any other girl, I'd drop her easily, but I couldn't drop Nina like that. She was too important to me for that. She'd become my world so easily with everything she was and even though I was so fucking pissed. I loved that girl with my entire heart.

Damn, I loved her.

AT THE SOFT knocks on my door, I opened it to find Nina there. She'd called and unable to live up to my promise, I answered her call. She wanted to see me, and I told her to come over when she had the chance.

I studied her as she stood at my door. She looked remorseful yet beautiful. I couldn't prolong the moment any longer and I pulled her into my arms, her face pressed against my chest for a moment.

With my arms wrapped around her, I held her as tight as I could. The days without her were torture. My entire schedule had been thrown. There was no picking her up from performances, talking about anything and everything, and kissing until we fell asleep together.

Leaving a kiss on the top of her head, I pulled her inside with me and walked her to the couch where I sat before pulling her into my lap. I pressed my lips to her neck and left a kiss.

"Ma petite danseuse," I muttered against her warm skin. "I'm sorry I blew up on you." It was the one thing I knew I needed to do, apologize. I was angry but my reaction was more than it should have been. Nina didn't deserve it.

"It's okay," she peered up at me, her warm brown eyes filled with anxious anticipation.

I knew it was her past relationship that left her in this meek place of letting someone treat her in contempt. I saw my father treat my mother like trash and take his anger over anything out on her. It wasn't okay.

"It's not okay," I asserted. "It is never okay. I shouldn't have blown up on you and expressed my anger like that. I'm so sorry."

"I accept your apology," she murmured.

I rubbed her back gently.

"I only hope you can understand. I'm not ready to tell my family about us."

I shook my head. Nina was a grown woman. Her parents couldn't stop us from what we had.

"I know you don't understand it. I just hope you understand enough," she began before taking a deep breath and glancing away from me. She looked down and played with her hands nervously. "My parents have only been truly proud of me once. The day I got married was the happiest day of their lives after my brother's marriage. I was following in line after going off course with my dancing. When I got divorced, they could never look at me the same again. They've always wanted one thing, for me to marry a strong African man, and to produce the next generation as was expected. I know my parents are old school, but all I've ever wanted was to make them proud."

"Even if that means giving up your own dreams and happiness," I commented as I thought of the conversation I had with Fabumi after I left the hospital. He expressed the same sentiment when it came to old school African families. Being the usual voice of reason, he's the one who calmed me down after I'd left to the gym to punch my anger out on some bags.

Nina's head rose and she gave an innocent shrug.

"Growing up, I never gave them reasons to be proud. I always fell short. I constantly fear falling shorter and shorter. My divorce was hard for them and now I can't just go and easily introduce you to them without some kickback. I want to be with you, I do, but if you can't work with me when it comes to my family then..." her voice trailed off as she glanced away.

"I'll be with you through fucking anything. I can promise you that, baby," I told her confidently. I wasn't going anywhere. If I had to be a secret to her family, I would have to accept that. "As long as I have you, I'm here." And then those words easily slipped from my mouth so quickly there was no taking them back, but I didn't want to take them back, ever. "I love you."

"I love you, too," she whispered with a grin on her face before I kissed her hard and with everything in me. She was mine unconditionally.

If anyone had defeated the Belgian Beast, it was Nina. I was at her will.

"Fuck, I've got to have you right now," I growled as I grabbed her in my arms and briskly carried her to my bedroom.

It had been over a week since I last had her there, but this time there would be no interruptions to our love making.

I stood her up before my bed and pulled off her sweater and shirt.

Nina stood in her black bra which I easily unhooked and pulled from her arms, leaving her completely topless as I bent down. I pressed my lips to her belly button, making her squirm as I unbuttoned and unzipped her jeans before dragging them with her panties down her legs.

Peering up at her gloriously slender, naked frame, I saw the innocent embarrassment in her eyes I saw our last time. I knew Nina was fairly religious and she wasn't one to give her body easily. This took thought and dedication I didn't take lightly. Nina was giving me a gift I'd cherish.

"Lay down," I instructed her, and she easily did as I told her and laid on my bed, her head settled on my pillows and she watched me while she bit down on her bottom lip nervously. "I'll be back."

With quick strides, I jolted into my bathroom to find my stash of condoms in the drawer. Gabbing one quickly, I rushed back into the bedroom where Nina patiently waited for me. I tossed the condom package onto the bed, eager to use it when the time came.

I yanked off my tank top and kicked my sweatpants off, leaving me bare like my girl. I took my cock into my hand and stroked it as I watched her watching me. She was intrigued and I was on fire at the sight of her lustful eyes.

"You want this cock, don't you, baby?" I asked gruffly as I climbed onto the bed with her. There was this vixen I saw behind Nina's hooded eyes when I talked dirty to her and I wanted to claw her out to bring her forward. "Or better, you want me to eat that pussy again. I remember the way you screamed for me last time. You liked it, didn't you?"

Bending over the bed and her, I ran my finger down her slit that was already glistening wet and showing me how much she craved it.

"Hmm, Nina?" I crawled up the bed and rose above her. I watched her chest move up and down with her shallow breaths as lowered my mouth and pulled one of her pebble hard dark chocolate tipped nipples into my mouth.

Sucking on her flesh, I listened to her soft moans before I moved to her other nipple and sucked it into my mouth, even grazing my teeth against her flesh pulling a gasp from her throat before I meticulously began to plant kisses down her stomach and over her inner thighs as I spread her legs.

Fingering open her folds, her wet and pink pussy stared back at me waiting to be satisfied by my tongue, my fingers, and my dick that was begging to get inside her again as it was far too short of a time last time.

"Tell me you liked it last time," I demanded.

"I *loved* it last time. Lick me, please," she said breathlessly, setting me on fucking fire.

Her wish was my command as I easily swirled my tongue over her clit while I pumped a couple of fingers into her. Her hips naturally began to ride against my hand and mouth while I pleasured her. With each lap, her sweet cream seeped into my mouth.

Fingernails dug into my bald scalp as her cries filled my ears. I stopped licking her and lifted my head as I kept fingering her, my thumb circling her clit as I watched her. Her body jolted under me.

"That's it, cum for me," I insisted as she did just that and came over my hand.

Grabbing the small foil package off the bed, I anxiously yanked it open before pulling out the condom and rolling it onto my hard and pulsing dick that was waiting so anxiously to be buried inside of Nina's soaking pussy.

I climbed over her and spread her legs a little wider. I allowed my finger to settle on her clit and gently rub circles around it to relax her as I began to sink into her.

"Fuck, you're so fucking tight," I grunted as I tried

my hardest to hang onto my load that was already threatening to spill out.

My arms took her into them and rolled over to put her on top. Nina's legs settled on either side of my hips as she began to roll her dancer's hips into mine. My eyes were almost crossed as she threw her head back and allowed her body to take over naturally. She was stunning as her braids dripped down her back and her dark tits bounced with the reflection of the streetlights dancing on them.

Her muscles were soon tightening around my cock, but I ached for it to last just a little bit longer. I couldn't cum in her just yet, there was so much more of where that came from. The full power of the Belgian Beast awaited her.

I pulled her off and she groaned in protest.

"On your stomach," I instructed. Nina nodded and laid on her stomach.

From behind her, I just barely lifted her hips and her heart shaped ass rose into the air. I cupped an ass cheek in my hand and squeezed it. With my other hand on my manhood, I slipped into her soaking pussy. Starting slowly at first, I rocked into her before those rocks because full on thrusts.

"Marc," she moaned into my pillow as my hand snaked around and the tips of my fingers found her clit once more. "Fuck!"

I rarely heard her swear. A smile spread across my lips knowing I'd made her throw away any inhibitions and purity.

Nina was getting every inch of my beast as I slammed into her harder, her screams filling my room with each hard thrust and slap of our bodies together before she tightened around me, and my balls went stiff. With a roar, I spilled into the condom, filling it while Nina cried satisfied wails into my pillow.

I waited until the pulsing of my cock slowed before I pulled out of her and rose from the bed. I staggered like a drunk man into the bathroom and took off the condom to dispose of it.

With my head spinning, I returned to the room and plopped onto the bed where a breathless Nina laid, and I pulled her into my arms, her round ass resting against my cock which was already straining for more of her even in my spent state. I kissed her shoulder before she turned to me. Her lips pressed to mine for a moment before she slightly pulled back and her eyes watched mine.

"I'm afraid every single day of you leaving me. I'm afraid of having you disappear," she confessed.

"Nothing will take me away from you. I'm here with you every single day and every step of the way. I told you I love you and I mean it from the bottom of my fucking heart. You are my heart," I told her and meant every word that left my mouth. She nodded and kissed me.

"I've never been loved before, not like this," she admitted.

"Get used to it, baby," I declared. "Get fucking used to it."

CHAPTER TEN

NINA

Putting away the final dish from my parent's dishwasher. I left the kitchen behind and strolled into the living room where I found my mother collapsed on the couch. She'd put Dad to bed while I finished the dishes.

My mother was always one to hold the family together, she was the pillar, but Dad was her right hand. With him weakened by his heart attack and subsequent surgery, Mom had been left to fare for everything on her own. I watched her rest for a moment before her eyes shot open at hearing me enter the room.

"Ma fille," she gave me a weak smile and patted the couch cushion next to her.

Fully entering the small family living room I crossed over and sat next to my mom who sat up a little and watched me.

"You seem different," she commented as she took my hand and squeezed it.

I give her a puzzled look wondering what she meant by *different*.

"In a good way. For so long, I watched you hang around with a frown on your face. You were never happy. I don't know what's changed but you're happy. I know one thing is for sure, seeing you happy makes me happy even with all that is going on."

"Thanks," I gave mom a smile.

It was true, I was happy. My fairly predictable life had taken such an unexpected turn when Marc entered it I honestly felt the difference. I spent less time secluded away in my apartment where I wallowed in my sorrows. For once, I was out in the world.

"A few nights ago, I was talking with your father. He told me one of his biggest fears when he had his heart attack was dying without seeing you married again, happy, and living. Honestly, I have the same fear, but seeing you smiling is a relief and a step forward. Now, if only we can settle you down with a good African man." Mom beamed at the prospect of having me settle again.

I cringed at the idea and wondered if my parents could accept Marc into our family as the man I settled down with. I loved him more than anything and being the woman he loved made me happier than I'd ever been.

Mom squeezed my hand again, tightly and I met her eyes again.

"You made a beautiful bride once and I think you'll make a beautiful one again. I can already imagine you with a round belly walking through here," she gushed with pride of a future I didn't exactly see for myself but it was what my parents wanted so deeply that anything less would keep me as a disappointment in their eyes.

"We'll see," I commented lightly in hopes we could end the conversation of the future they wanted to impose upon me as they'd done before.

"Ayo says you two are going to New York. What for?" Mom asked as she looked me over. I knew that look. She would give it to me as a kid when she knew I was plotting something that wasn't exactly something she wanted me part of.

I shrugged slightly as if to dismiss the whole thing as not a big deal. It really was a huge deal. Marc was fighting another high-profile American fighter. He was representing not just himself and Jean in the United States but representing Belgium in a huge way. He was already known worldwide but this would show the world who he was on a much bigger stage.

"I have to go to New York for work," I lied through my teeth. I hated lying to my parents, but it was the only way to keep them off my back. In most things I couldn't be truthful with them. Even when I was on the edge and at my most depressed, I would play it off on sickness or a simple headache when it was always much more, when I was falling apart at the seams.

"I'm seeing some pretty influential dancers in the ballet scene perform and I thought Ayo would be a good companion." That part was true. With the chance of going to New York, I immediately got my hands on tickets to the ballet and Ayo was always the perfect person to take on an adventure of any sort.

Mom rubbed my arm gently before she spoke. "Be careful. I'm glad you're taking someone with you. I hope to hear about your trip when you get back. I know Ayo is going to soak up New York City."

I laughed. Ayo was ecstatic about the trip. He'd already planned out an entire itinerary around our trip. He wanted to see all the big landmarks like Times Square and The Statue of Liberty, as well as hit up all the trendy bars and nightclubs.

"It will be a good trip," I mentioned, not spilling the real reason behind it but knowing I would have the time of my life with the man I loved.

"There are a lot of African men there, maybe you can pick up a husband while you're there and move to America. That would be a dream, wouldn't it?" Mom gave me a wink.

I provided a weak smile at her sentiment, she meant well at least.

FROM THE MOMENT the plane landed, I ached to see Marc after being without him for a week. He'd gone ahead to New York with Jean a week before the fight. Ayo, Fabumi, Emmy, and I travelled together to support Marc.

Emmy led the way through the airport having travelled through New York many times before. Though being born and bred in Belgium, Emmy was a US citizen. Her mother was African American and her father Belgian. Emmy frequently returned to the US to visit her American family.

Following Emmy, who pushed a stroller with her and Fabumi's newborn, we exited into the International Arrivals corridor. My heart pumped and butterflies fluttered as my eyes scanned the crowd for Marc and they landed directly on the tall, bald man with shining eyes who held my heart.

Not caring what any onlooker thought, a first for me, I broke into a run before I dropped my bag and jumped into his arms. With my legs wrapped around his waist, he crushed his mouth to mine and kissed me hard.

"I missed you so fucking much, ma petite danseuse," he grumbled against my lips before kissing me again to the whistles of onlookers. I grinned proudly at the simple thought that I was his girl and there was this man waiting for me.

"Okay lovebirds, Allons-y," Fabumi chuckled from behind us before Marc put me down. He picked up my bag and followed along to the van waiting for all of us.

Marc and I spent the ride to the hotel completely in one another. I hung on his every word as he talked about the interviews he'd done over the week and meeting the other fighters at a promotional event where he came head to head with his opponent who sounded like a piece of work, but I knew Marc could handle him.

There were only three days until the fight, and I could feel Marc's normally calm demeanor was a little more intensified. When it came to fighting, he took every moment seriously and I respected that as I was the same about dance.

"Are you ready to see New York?" He played with my freshly done braids.

"Of course," I cooed as his hand rubbed my thigh. I slapped a hand over my mouth as I yawned. "Maybe, a nap first though."

"Auntie did send me with a mission," Ayo piped up from the seat behind us.

"And that was?" I was afraid of what mission my mother gave my cousin for our trip to the Big Apple.

"To find you a husband," he laughed.

"Is that so?" Marc asked as he turned in the direction of Ayo who continued with his fit of laughter over the matter. "I guess you have a wingman." Marc nudged my shoulder with his own with a snicker before putting his arm around me.

I instantly folded my arms.

"It's not funny," I shot at them. I didn't want to talk about my inability to be fully open and honest about my relationship with Marc because it put this dark cloud over us. I wouldn't bring that into our trip.

"I'm sorry, mon amour," Marc whispered into my ear before kissing my cheek. I turned my head to face his and kissed his lips. "I've missed this all week. I'm so glad you're here."

"Me too."

THE MUSIC PUMPED through our bodies as we danced. After a little resting, a fighter friend of Marc invited our group out to a local popular nightclub. Marc was quick after a couple drinks to pull me onto the dance floor. We were living our best and carefree lives while in New York.

Marc's hands were all over my body, worshipping every bit he could with my clothes on. I leaned into him, my ass bouncing against his dick that was straining at his jeans. I couldn't wait for us to be back in the hotel room, alone.

I glanced over to see my cousin flirting with a guy he'd met as soon as we got to the club, and Fabumi sitting pretty in VIP with Emmy on his lap. Emmy was eager for a night out after being sequestered at home with their newborn. Her aunt didn't live too far from the city and came out to babysit for the evening to give the new parents a well-deserved break.

"Let's get some air," Marc said into my ear over the loud music.

I responded with a nod as he laced our fingers together and we weaved through the grinding bodies of the dance floor and out onto a balcony.

Marc leaned onto the railing and pulled me into his

arms, I rested my chin on his chest as I peered up at him. Before, I was never one to be in the middle of a dance floor at any night club unless Ayo had physically dragged me there with him.

I had this confidence in myself I'd only ever felt when dancing. It poured through me like an open dam. I stood taller in a way I'd never done. I was inching toward more control. The only thing I lacked was the ability to stand up to my parents in who I wanted to be with.

"I'm having the best time," I expressed wholeheartedly and a little breathlessly as I came down from all the dancing.

"Good." Marc kissed my forehead before I stood on the tips of my toes and kissed his warm lips. "Are you excited for the ballet tomorrow?"

"I'm beyond excited," I gushed at the buzz of seeing my idol, Misty Copeland, live on stage and embodying what it was not to just be a ballerina, but one of color. Just getting my hands on tickets was thrilling in itself.

Marc twirled my braids with his hand as he tended to do. I leaned into him and pressed my head to his chest, listening to his heart thump under my ear.

"Seeing you excited and happy is everything I could ask for," Marc continued to toy with my hair. "It's all I want."

"What?"

"Your happiness."

"Lookie here, there goes baldy again," a voice in English cut through the moment.

I ignored it as we were in a busy nightclub and it could be directed at anyone.

"This fucker," Marc grumbled under his breath and I turned to see a guy approaching us.

He was about as tall as Marc and incredibly muscular, almost inhuman like in the way they bulged from his shirt. The guy's dark hair was flopped over to one side. He approached us with an entourage of guys and a sneer on his ugly face.

Marc secured his arm around my waist and held me tight. I felt his heart-rate accelerate, and his stance stiffen as he stood taller.

"Having a little fun before I kick your ass on Saturday, huh, Little Belgian?" The guy asked with a condescending snarl to his voice.

I scrunched my face and furrowed my brow. I wanted to fight him myself.

"And you've got a little bitch to keep you company."

"Fuck yourself, Bartowski," Marc hissed angrily, his Belgian accent strong as he spoke in English. "Leave my girlfriend out of this."

"Girlfriend?" Bartowski questioned with a smirk as he stepped closer and reached out a hand that just barely grazed my face when Marc slapped it away. "Nice little monkey you've got." Bartowski snickered and his guys joined in laughing.

I was shaking and Marc pushed me behind him as he stepped in Bartowski's face on the ready attack. It was almost possible to see the steam coming from his ears.

"Apologize," Marc growled.

"For what?" The men were face to face and people all around had caught wind of what was going on. Phones were out and recording the confrontation while I stood by helpless.

"Piece of shit. I'm going to tear you the fuck apart on Saturday," Marc affirmed as security arrived and tried their hardest to break the men apart, but neither would budge. They were screaming insults at one another and trying to get in hits.

I rushed to Marc and touched his shoulder.

He peered back at me and his eyes immediately met mine.

"Please, Marc. Let's go," I pleaded in French.

Marc nodded in response and turned away as the bigger person. He laced his fingers with mine and we began to walk back into the club to get the rest of our group when Bartowski shouted a few insults that made Marc pause for a moment. His breathing was heavy, ragged, but I gripped tightly to his hand to keep his anger from overflowing.

"That's right, walk away like the little bitch you are. You and your little nigger whore!" Bartowski shouted over the crowd and music.

Marc dropped my hand and in seconds he was barreling toward Bartowski.

I stood unable to do anything. With my small frame I could never hold back my beast of a boyfriend who was pissed beyond all reason. Marc was a bear defending his territory with a feoricity I'd never seen another person display before. I stood horrified as the men went at it. My heart thumped in my throat and it felt as if it would burst out of my body. I had no way of stopping the disaster that unfolded in front of my eyes.

"Marc, arrête s'il-te-plaît!" I screamed at the top of my lungs as if he could hear me over it all.

Justin, Marc's friend who'd invited us out, and a few other fighters all rushed from the club and worked to pull the men apart. My entire body was shaking intensely as I watched him yank Marc from on top of Bartowski. Justin and Marc stumbled back together, tripping over a table and chairs but caught themselves before falling.

Marc attempted to jump back into the fray but was held back by Justin and two other guys.

"Nina, can you calm him down?" Justin asked me anxiously as he struggled to keep Marc under any control.

I stood still in my spot in a haze of shock.

"Please, Nina, we need your help."

"Go to him, I'll get Emmy and Fabumi," Ayo's voice came into my ear and I turned to see my wide-eyed cousin with the guy he'd been flirting with next to him.

"Okay," I sprinted to Marc and placed a hand on his arm.

Getting my first look at his face, he had blood gushing from his nose and a busted lip. I swallowed away my aversion to blood.

"Marc let's go. Come on, please," I begged him as he continued to fight the guys and raged on. "Marc!" I screeched at the top of my lungs and his eyes snapped into mine. "Let's go calm down."

Marc didn't say a single word to me or anyone else as he stepped in my direction. Someone handed me a towel which I quickly gave to Marc who put his arm around my waist and walked with me.

As we stepped through the club, patrons parted and made a pathway for us. Fabumi, Emmy, and Ayo were all at the door.

"Holy fuck," Fabumi commented at the sight of him, who's only response was grunted.

"Let's go!" Marc barked at us.

I swallowed hard as a tear fell down my cheek.

Ayo rushed to my side and wrapped an arm around me as Marc led the way out of the club.

My heart thumped at Marc becoming another person when provoked. It was so much like the character of my ex-husband who'd transform from a very chill guy to a monster easily. I didn't want to be afraid of Marc but right then and there, I was.

CHAPTER ELEVEN

MARC

It was a pure miracle I wasn't disqualified after the fight in the club. There was no way to explain it besides I saw red and went for Bartowski hard. I could deal with him insulting me and trying to rile me up, but when it came to Nina, I wouldn't let him—or anyone—talk shit.

Yet, when it came to Nina, it backfired on me. I saw the fear deep in her eyes whenever she looked at me the rest of the night. She wouldn't even sleep with me and moved into Ayo's room for the night. I'd failed her and that was the biggest defeat I could ever face.

"How was the ballet?" I asked as she stepped into the front doors of the hotel with Ayo by her side.

"Good," she answered in one word and kept walking toward the hotel elevators with her cousin. *Fuck*.

"Good news, the fight will still happen tomorrow

night," I informed her as I sprinted to keep up with her quick pace.

"Hmm." That wasn't even a full word.

Fuck. Fuck! I'd never fucked up so bad before and my heart pumped with what the outcome could be. I refused to lose her. Nina was everything my life required in it. I jogged to keep up with her as she kept moving.

"Mon chéri." I placed a hand on her shoulder to slow her pace. She froze and her eyes scanned me over and there it was again, that fear. I swallowed hard and how surprisingly emotional I got when I looked into her warm, yet afraid eyes. "Can we talk?"

"I don't think that's a good idea," her voice was quiet, and it burned hearing her sound so small.

"I know I don't deserve it but give me a chance, baby. I made a mistake last night. I let my anger get the best of me and I acted like an animal. You know I'm better than that, don't you?" I asked just hoping it would give me a lifeline with her. Even if she only gave me a moment, I'd make that moment last forever because I needed her forever.

"Marc," she started. I prayed silently that it wouldn't be the end. It could be the end between us. "I'd rather talk upstairs if that's okay."

"Oui, Mon chéri. Anything for you to be comfortable," I groveled. I wasn't the groveling and begging type, but if I was going to possibly lose the woman I loved, I'd be on my hands and knees begging for her to stay with me and I'd have no shame doing it.

The three of us stepped into the elevator. Ayo pressed the button for the floor we were all staying on and the doors closed, leaving us in an eerie silence. No one said a word as the elevator climbed floors and with a ding the doors opened to our floor.

I allowed both Nina and Ayo out in front of me.

"I'll see you soon," Nina said to her cousin who gave her a reassuring nod before she turned to face me and motioned for me to lead the way to the room which was supposed to be ours but instead I was left to sleep alone.

She followed behind me.

My heartbeat grew louder in my ears with every step toward the room at the end of the hall. I pulled the keycard from my pocket and opened the door. With a wave of my hand, I motioned for Nina to step inside. She entered the room and I followed, the door closing behind me with a click.

"You said the ballet was good?" I questioned innocently, making small talk before we got right into the matter.

Nina sat on the edge of the bed and crossed her legs. She didn't say a word and clearly wasn't entertained by my small talk.

I ran my hand over my bald head as I sat down next to her.

"Last night," she began as she looked down at her hands in her lap. "I didn't know who you were anymore. You weren't Marc, my protector, the man I loved. You turned into this monster. It's like I discovered why they call you the Belgian Beast. You were a beast last night who was out for the kill. The rage and fury I saw sent me right back to when I was married and my husband would turn from one man into another, a raging monster let out of his cage. Those were the times he hurt me the most."

"But I'd never hurt you, Nina. You know that, right?" I asked as I lifted her chin and she looked at me, really looked at me for the first time.

"I want to say yes. I really do but je ne sais pas." She was physically shaking as she sat next to me.

My heart shattered knowing I gave her this reaction. I wasn't that man. I wasn't like her ex-husband, nor my father. I'd never hit a woman especially the woman I loved.

"Nina," I whispered not really having the words anymore. Even knowing I wasn't, I felt like I was a monster.

Small sobs began to erupt from her as she quaked next to me.

I wrapped my arms around her and held her close without words.

She needed to let all the fear she'd held in, come out.

I wouldn't stop her from her moment but be there with her as she went through it. To me, that was my number one job. I had to support her through it all, even when it was harder than I could imagine.

"I was so scared," she cried onto my chest.

"Merde," I cursed under my breath. "Je suis désolé.

You should never be afraid because of me. Never," I proclaimed as I continued to hold her in my arms. I had so much to work on as a man but even more so as the one who was the protector of Nina's heart. I was a better man than that and I was committed to showing that.

After a few minutes, Nina pulled away slightly and looked up at me. Her make-up was smudged, and black streaks fell down her cheeks. Never again would I allow her to feel that way. Never again would I contribute to her tears, and never again would she have to face the fear of any man.

"Are we going to be okay?" I was desperate to know if I'd ever get that chance with her again. I'd walked alone for so long and to have her by my side was another universe and I didn't want to go back to how things were. Life without her spark wasn't life at all.

"Nina," I hummed as I placed a finger under her chin and brought her closer. "I love you."

"I love you too. That was the hardest part of it. Seeing the man I love become…" her voice trailed off.

"A monster, I know. I guess there's a reason they call me the Belgian Beast, but I promise I'll never be that man around you. I fucking promise it with everything," I swore.

"Can you make me another promise?" Her lips hovered barely a centimeter from my own which were aching to kiss her.

"Anything, ma petite danseuse."

"Tomorrow night, kick that piece of shit's ass."

I laughed loudly before I crushed my mouth to hers ignoring the wincing pain in my busted lip. I lost myself in the kiss. Greedily claiming her as I laid us on the bed. Her leg wrapped around me, pulling me in close as her hands gripped at my shirt.

"You're. So. Fucking. Amazing," I said between kisses as I pulled her over me, letting her hips straddle mine.

My hand traveled under the hem of her dress and gripped onto her panty covered ass. I needed her out of her panties as soon as possible. Every part of my body burned to have her flesh connected with mine, to hear her screams of pleasure, and to hold her as if today was the beginning of forever.

Sliding under the elastic of her underwear, my fingers found her clit and began to stroke it between her folds that grew wetter with each stroke of my digits.

"Marc," Nina gasped into my mouth as her hips bucked into my hand. She was just as desperate for me as I was for her.

"Tell me, Nina," I grumbled to her. "Why is your pussy so wet?"

"You," she gasped as I pinched her clit between my thumb and forefinger.

Gripping her panties, we maneuvered together, and it wasn't long before I had them sliding down her legs and she was kicking them off. My hands gripped her hips knowing exactly where I wanted her. I lifted her as I slid down the bed and her soaked pussy was just above my mouth.

Unable to wait any longer, I pulled her down and began licking her warm center. My tongue darting in and out as she rode my face. Her knees tightening around my head muffled my hearing, but I could still hear Nina's cries into the room as she filled my mouth with her sweet explosion.

The beast in my pants throbbed with eager excitement to be buried inside her, feeling her, and loving her for every bit she was.

I laid Nina on the bed, she glanced up at me, her eyes glazed over in ecstasy. Bending to her, I began to undo the buttons of her flowing dress. With each small button I did away with, a small bit of her deeply toasted flesh was exposed to me. Soon she laid under me, her body exposed as she hadn't worn a bra with her backless dress.

Standing straight up, I tore off my shirt and ripped my usual sweatpants down my legs to be just as bare as her.

Bending to her stomach, I planted a kiss on her belly button and left a trail of small kisses up the center of her chest to her perky breasts that awaited me. I took one nipple into my mouth while I pinched the other between my fingers. I needed all of her, and I'd take her one moment at a time.

"Shit," I grumbled as I reluctantly pulled myself away from her body. I stumbled to my suitcase and dug through until I found exactly what I was looking for.

Grabbing the condom, I made quick work of getting it open and sliding it onto my rock-hard dick.

Unable to wait any longer I pounced onto the bed and spread her legs and sunk into her in one swift motion. Filling her, I pulled out and slammed back into her. Our eyes locked and I refused to lose her heated gaze while I made love to her.

Nina's legs wrapped around my waist and her fingernails dug into my shoulders as she pulled me in as close as she could get me.

Our breathing was heavy as our slick bodies rode into one another. With the pressure building in my stomach, I tried to keep going as long as I could, my deep groans echoing through the room with Nina's whimpers.

Reaching the brink, I reached down and pressed my thumb to Nina's throbbing bud. Her body began to shake under me as her muscles squeezed my cock tight.

"I'm cuming," she cried, her nails likely breaking the skin on my back as she dug them in deep.

"That's it, come on my cock," I growled as my own orgasm struck and I thrust into her harder, the pulsing rolling through from my dick to my brain until I felt a release and a different sensation.

I allowed my high to fall before I pulled out of her. The cold air shook me back to reality as I shot my head down to see the tip of my cock had broken through the rubber of the condom.

"Fuck, fuck," I cursed in a panic.

"What's wrong?" Nina asked concerned as she pulled herself up on her elbows.

"The condom broke," I confessed as my heart thumped out of my chest and I watched the horror flash through Nina's own eyes.

Nina took a deep breath before she placed a hand on mine and gave me a weak smile.

"This might sound crazy but if it is God's will, then it is." There was this calmness she brought over the room. Normally, and with any other girl I would have lost my shit, but Nina put us both at ease. I never saw myself as a father, but suddenly I thought, maybe.

"Are you sure, mon chéri?" I asked as I removed the broken condom and tossed it in the trash before I sat on the edge of the bed and pulled Nina into my arms.

Nina nodded with a smile on her face and kissed me. She pulled away and stared at my face for a moment. "I don't know. I sound crazy, right?"

I rubbed my hand over the smooth skin of her shoulder and upper arm savoring the feel of her close to me.

"It's like you said, nothing is chance, there's always a purpose. You're in my life for a reason and this happened for a reason. Maybe it's meant to be."

"Peut être," I muttered.

"I don't know," she laughed for a moment. "This isn't me, but I like her. It's like I'm becoming the person I should have always been. Maybe that girl is a mother. Maybe she's happy with you. Maybe she's free."

"With me, you'll always be free."

"Always?"
"Always."

THE EXHILARATION RUSHED through me from head to toe and every limb as I entered the octagon. The cage had been my home since I was fifteen. I'd gone from some kid who won a few fights to a champion with a reputation to uphold. The Belgian Beast would remain undefeated.

The feeling of Nina's lips lingered on mine from the last kiss she gave me before I was off to get ready for this very moment. She was somewhere in a box being waited on hand and foot while she waited for the end of the fight. Nina wouldn't watch, but she was here with me and that's what mattered.

"Nathan Bartowski!" I heard my opponents name announced and I saw him emerge. We both looked like shit from our fight in the nightclub. My lip was busted, and I had a black eye. Bartowski also sported a shiner and had some cuts on his face.

Bartowski sneered at me, his royal blue mouthguard staring back at me. He had no idea what I had in store for him. Last night, he'd done more than talk shit, he disrespected the woman I love, and for that alone he'd fucking pay. He could spout off any shit he wanted about me, but Nina was strictly off limits.

It was almost a blur. At the bell, I rushed him. I didn't have time for games and dancing around the cage. I had business to handle and I'd fucking handle it. I blocked his kick toward my face. I grabbed his leg and dropped him to the ground. The roar of the crowd was pure fire that burned through me and egged me on.

Growls and grunts pierced the air as I took him to the ground. I swear we'd only been in the cage for under a minute and we were already on the ground and I laid punch after punch into his face as I did last night.

Suddenly, he somehow snagged me and took control using one of his legs around my arm. I heard an unmistakable snap, but I didn't let that stop me. I couldn't use that arm, but I still had another. I got out of his hold and pressed my knee to his chest. I punched him directly in the face until I saw the moment I had seen plenty of times before, his eyes rolled back in his head and it was done.

Standing, a ferocious roar ripped through my body as I pounded my chest in victory. The Belgian Beast remained undefeated. As the ref took my arm to claim me the winner, I let out a scream as pain ricocheted from my arm, up through my entire body.

"Fuck!" I growled as I realized my arm was broken.

Pain clouded my vision and I could barely see the outline of Jean as he joined me in the cage along with whom I assumed were medics. My heart thumped loudly in my chest while they stabilized my arm in a splint and injected me with a painkiller.

The entire ceremony of receiving my belt was a

blur and as soon as it was over, I was rushed out a back entrance to a waiting ambulance with Jean with me.

"Nina," I moaned as I tried to keep my arm as steady as possible.

"She's with the others. We'll check your situation at the hospital and let her know what's going on. Don't worry, she'll stay informed," Jean slapped my good arm in reassurance. I nodded as I tried not to focus on the throbbing pain. "You did good, kid. The arm is a little bit of a setback, but you'll be back in no time."

"I think I want to ask Nina to marry me," I spouted the words at once. Hell, I hadn't even seen them coming. Maybe it was the painkillers bringing out my deepest thoughts.

"Holy shit, do you think you're ready for that? You haven't even known her long." Jean was taken aback at my outburst.

"I know but somehow I know it's right. There is only one problem," I remembered suddenly, and it threw a damper on my entire plan.

"What's that?" Jean asked now intrigued by everything.

"Her family. They don't even know about me and it's pretty much a given that they won't accept me. Nina's so afraid of how they'll react but I love her and I'm not giving her up. Never," I declared it fully.

Hell, there was a chance she could be having my baby.

CHAPTER TWELVE

NINA

Pacing the hospital waiting room, my head snapped toward the door at any sign of life coming in. My heart pounded in worry as we waited for news of how Marc had fared during surgery to place pins in his broken arm.

I refused to watch the fight. As much as I wanted to watch Marc kick the shit out of Bartowski, I couldn't dare watch it. Luckily, our group had been given a box for the event. I spent my time eating snacks, chatting with Emmy, and watching a movie on the television. When Fabumi informed me of Marc's win, I left my place on the couch and stepped to the glass where I saw Marc in the middle of the octagon, and he was screaming in obvious pain.

The three of us were rushed out and Fabumi contacted Jean who told us they were headed to the hospital. Getting there for me was a blur. I was on edge and afraid of what an injury could mean for him.

Marc's career was everything for him, it was his therapy, as dancing was for me.

Arriving at the hospital, I was allowed to be with him while the swelling went down until it was time for him to be wheeled into the operating room for surgery.

"Nina, sit, Chouchou," Ayo instructed from where he was seated on the highly uncomfortable plastic chairs. I frowned and skulked in his direction before I sat down with him. "He's going to be fine."

"I know," I huffed as I glanced up at the clock. I was exhausted from still being jet lagged and not having any sleep. "It's taking so long."

"The doctor did say it could take a few hours. He's going to be okay," Ayo tried to remind me. I knew he would be fine, but my heart hurt to have him hurt.

The chair next to me squeaked and I glanced over to Jean who'd taken the seat next to me. The older man who I didn't know terribly well gave me a weak smile before taking my hand into his and squeezing it tight. I knew he meant a lot to Marc and vice versa and had an almost Father-Son connection.

"I had my doubts in the beginning," Jean began as he looked forward and at the posters on the opposite wall about flu shots, STD protection, and pregnancy prevention. I wanted to snicker at the irony. "Marc has had women in and out of his life but never anyone who's come in and transformed him into a man who's ready to lay it all on the line. Hell, it's a first, seeing him in love, and I'm pretty damn sure you love him too."

"I do," I felt the tears prickling in the corners of my

eyes. Life without Marc was unimaginable. We were so incredibly different but alike at the same time. We meshed in a way I'd never expected to mesh with another person.

"Good, he needs it and will need it. It's going to take him some time to heal and I know it's going to be a hit to him mentally. Yes, he won the fight, but I think he'll begin to feel defeated. With you, he'll have someone to keep his spirits up and motivate him. He's got a long road ahead of him," Jean expressed.

There weren't any doubts in my mind. I'd be there to support Marc as he'd supported me. When I needed to cry, rage, and purge, he'd been there through it all. Our short season together was destined to turn into many seasons and possible years.

"I'm looking for the family of Marc Vandenberghe," a voice called from the door in crisp American English.

We all put our focus on the doctor in scrubs who stood at the door of the waiting room. He had a smile on his face and I immediately took it as good news. My heart thumped a little less hard as we all stood and scrambled to the doctor.

"I'm Marc's trainer," Jean answered to the man. "This is his girlfriend," he pointed over to me. "How's Marc?"

"He's good. We were able to get the pins in. He's stable and in recovery. I will have a report of the surgery ready for him to take back to his doctors in Belgium. He has some healing time ahead of him but with time well spent and physical therapy after, I think he'll be fighting again. Go Belgian Beast!" The doctor cheered proudly.

I giggled as the doctor was clearly an MMA fan.

Jean thanked the doctor while Ayo gave me a hug from behind. It was going to be good. There were unknowns about our future, but we'd face them together, it was the only way. As long as we were together, I was happy.

―――

WAITING for the timer to alarm was nerve racking. I swallowed the small bit of saliva I had in my mouth hard as I was parched from the anticipation. In the weeks since New York, I was anxious for what was possibly in store for Marc and I. Returning to Belgium, I felt much as I had when I'd gotten pregnant during my marriage. I just knew I was and when I missed my period, it was the sign I needed to finally take a test.

"I don't see how you can just sit there so calmly," I fussed in Marc's direction as he lay on the bed, propped up with a pillow, his arm in a sling as it had been since we'd returned home.

Marc chuckled at my frazzled state. I'd been so calm until the moment after I peed on the stick minutes ago. It was possible that everything could change, and it hit me that as much as I wanted it, I wasn't exactly ready.

"Come here," Marc summoned me to him with a pat on his lap.

Healing wasn't easy for him. He spent the first days

in immense pain. Now he was mostly frustrated he couldn't train how he liked and getting around on his motorbike was impossible. He was used to doing things around his house without assistance, but he needed help, which drove him crazy.

Shuffling to the bed, I took my spot right next to Marc and laid my head on his chest. Using his good arm, he stroked my face and left a kiss on the top of my head.

I glanced over to the pile of my clothes on top of my mostly unpacked suitcase that was building in the corner of his room and grinned. Since returning from the US, I'd been staying with Marc, only going home to check my mail and pick up new clothes when needed.

"We're going to have to clean out my closet to make room for your stuff," Marc noted as he'd noticed me checking out the mess I'd created in his normally neat room. "Or we can just find a new place for us and the little one." He placed his only usable hand on my flat but bloated stomach and rubbed.

"Mmm, how would you feel about moving outside the city. A little house in the countryside for the three of us," I mentioned casually as I smiled up at Marc.

"Sounds perfect to me. I love Bruxelles, I grew up here, but a change would be nice. Fabumi and Emmy just bought a place in Enghien, it's a place to look." Marc had sat back, his head on the headboard as he dreamed up a look at our future as a family.

"That's closer to my family…" My voice trailed as my family entered my mind. They didn't even know about Marc and me. If I was pregnant, I knew they could never forgive me.

"You'll have to tell them about us," Marc reminded me.

I grimaced at the idea. I wasn't ready to be disowned for possibly getting pregnant out of wedlock, and then with a man who wasn't African. If it were any other time in history I would be burned at the stake.

"We can't keep us a secret forever."

"Why can't we?" I whined clearly knowing it wasn't realistic but not brave enough to go there yet. "I don't want to talk about it right now, please."

"Nina, we can't keep ignoring it. It's going to have to eventually happen."

"Je sais."

"Then let's figure out how," Marc argued.

"Arrêtez! I said I'm done talking about it," I fussed before the alarm tone of my phone interrupted us.

At lightning speed, I shot out of Marc's arm and jolted into the bathroom with my heart pounding out of my chest. I could heart Marc's feet padding across the wood flooring until he arrived at the entrance to his bathroom.

Peering over at him, I took a deep breath before I approached the counter fully and looked directly down at the white and blue pregnancy test staring back at me with YES+ on the screen. My thumping heart stopped as I gasped and turned to face Marc who was now directly behind me with the biggest and cheesiest grin on his face. His good arm looped around me and he easily picked me up.

"We're having a baby!" He cheered as he swung me around in excitement.

"Put me down," I laughed. "I don't want you getting hurt."

Setting me back on my feet, Marc got down on his knees and pressed his lips to my stomach.

"You have no idea the gift you're giving me," he muttered as he glanced up into my eyes, piercing through me with such pride. "No fucking idea. I never expected to be a father and as much as the idea scares me, I think I can handle it. I had a pretty damn good example of what not to do. I'm never going to be that man. I'm going to be the best man my child can have." A single tear fell down Marc's face.

"I love you," I whispered as I cupped his cheek and wiped his tears away. "I wouldn't want to have a child with any other man. Only you."

―――

MY STOMACH TURNED at the smell of food as soon as I entered my parent's house. I tried to swallow away my budding nausea which had become a staple in my life in the last few days. My mornings and sometimes late evenings were filled with Marc using his good hand to hold my hair back while I bent over the toilet and allowed my stomach to empty.

"You are looking a little gray, Nina," my mother

mentioned as I took a seat in the living room where Dad was parked in his favorite armchair as had become the usual with him still healing from his heart attack and surgery.

Everyday Dad was stronger, which was a good sign, but he wasn't out of danger. Mom was doing a good job at changing up his diet even though he fought her on it, and she made him take a small walk around the block every evening to get in some exercise.

A small boy climbed into my lap and snuggled onto my leg. My nephew, Malik, sucked his thumb as he studied my face. I could hear his siblings in the next room playing as they usually were. My old bedroom at my parent's home had been turned into a playroom for my brother's children and maybe my own if they didn't hate me when they found out my secret.

"I made a little salad. Do you want some Nina?" Mom asked.

"No, merci," I answered as I thought about the salad I'd vomited up immediately after dinner last night.

"Are you sure you aren't sick?" Mom asked concerned as she stepped to me and pressed her hand to my forehead.

"I'm fine, maman, my stomach is just a little upset," I argued in annoyance. "Où sont Jaheem and Suzanna?" I quickly changed the subject as I noticed my brother and sister-in-law hadn't arrived yet. The little boy on my lap was grabbing at my face. I smiled at him and poked his little nose to have him fall into a fit of giggles.

"Suzanna had a doctor's appointment. They should be here soon," my mom mentioned as she rubbed my nephew's small head. "It's looking like another baby for them."

"Wow," I commented. I wasn't really looking forward to being pregnant at the same time as my sister-in-law who was always an attention seeking handful whenever she was with child but maybe it was a positive to me. Her attention whore ways would deflect everyone's attention away from me.

My first appointment was just after the weekend and I was anxious for it. I'd gone through the first fifteen weeks of pregnancy before. The last time I wasn't quite as filled with joy. I was living in a state of fear of what my husband would and could do to me. This time would be different. I had Marc.

"One day you'll be joining Suzanna," Dad mentioned with a proud grin. "You'll be a good mother. You had the best example." Dad beamed as he looked over to my mom. I always adored their love. They were one another's backbone and so much of how they were reminded me of myself and Marc.

"Nous sommes là!" Suzanna's voice announced her and my brother's arrival at the front door.

"Maman! Papa!" The voices of the children in the other room began to cheer in excitement. I could hear their little feet stomping off toward the front door to find their arriving parents.

Only a few moments later, my brother and sister-in-law entered the living room with children clinging to them. They greeted my parents first, Suzanna gave me a listless greeting as she picked up her youngest from my arms before my brother picked me up as he always did.

"Wow, you're getting heavy," Jaheem mentioned as he placed me back on my feet.

"She is looking a little fuller, isn't she?" Mom questioned as my brother examined my face. My weight of course was the topic the of evening but this time I was bigger. Things didn't change much around my family home.

"Those cheeks are getting fluffy. What have you been eating?" He asked jokingly.

I simply shrugged innocently and gave a fake chuckle at the invasive question. I was going to have to tell them at some point. Everything would have to be revealed and the thought of it made me shiver with anxiety. Suddenly, the contents of my stomach were in my throat. I yanked away from my brother and sprinted up the hall toward the bathroom. Shutting myself inside, I bent over the toilet and let everything go.

"Nina, are you sure you aren't sick?" Mom asked from the bathroom door.

"I'm fine," I answered quickly before heaving up another helping of bile into the toilet.

"You'd think she was pregnant or something," I could hear Suzanna joke from the other room. I froze suddenly at my sister-in-law's words. Telling them now would be too much. I knew the outcome. I knew that my parents would disavow me. It would be a mess. I wasn't married and I was pregnant. I'd committed sin.

Those thoughts bubbled inside me. Growing legs like an invasive spider that trickled from my mind and through my veins. They filled me with their venom that sent me into a place I knew well.

Standing up, I rinsed my mouth and leaned against the cabinet with my hand over my belly as I tried to fight my anxiety away. Glancing at myself in the mirror, I could only see my perceived sin sticking to me.

It seemed as if out of the blue, my face was covered in sweat, my heart palpitated quickly, and I trembled as I gripped onto the counter and held on. Another anxiety attack was rocking me to my core easily. They'd picked up as of late. I hated feeling out of control but there was nothing I could do about it. The worst was when there was no warning and out of the blue they rocked and rolled through me.

Mom was talking to me through the door, but I didn't have it in me to pay attention to her words. I rubbed my belly and worked to steady my breathing. We had an adventure ahead of us. I didn't know how my family would take it, but I couldn't hide it forever as much as I kind of wanted to.

CHAPTER THIRTEEN

MARC

Grunting, I punched the leather bag with force. I only had one arm to do it, but I was determined to not just sit around and waste precious time. I was healing, yes, but I still had a level of fitness to maintain until the cast could come off my arm in another couple of weeks. The waiting was brutal and mentally I felt like a failure.

"A waste of space." My father's voice haunted me more and more. I couldn't fight and not being able to get in the octagon made me feel like the loser he'd always pegged me to be.

As he taunted me, I jabbed the bag harder and harder. I needed to fight his voice away as I normally did, but it wasn't happening, he stayed present.

"You could never be half the man I am. You're just a pussy," he jeered through my head.

I wanted to scream in his face I was a much better man than him and I'd raise my children without the trauma he inflicted upon me and Sophie. My child would never know the fear I grew up with. My child would have a meal on the table every night and the safe arms of his or her father.

My child.

Whenever I thought of the child Nina was carrying, I was filled with this joy I always thought was unattainable, but now I had it. The woman I'd been with for only a matter of months was giving me a gift I could never truly thank her for.

For both of us, our lives had taken a different direction than we could ever predict, but we were both incredibly grateful to have one another and this chance to bring a person into the world. My only gripe was Nina still refused to tell her family about us. It had become the only thing we fought about.

I tried to not push her on it too much as she'd become increasingly panicked about it, but the waiting was getting harder. I didn't see any shame in us nor that we'd made a life together, but Nina felt tremendous shame I could never understand.

"I thought I'd find you here," the sweetest voice cut through my concentration and I turned to find her staring at me. "I just finished getting my hair done. Do you like it?" Nina did a little twirl showing off her freshly done braids.

"Beautiful," I murmured as I approached her and wrapped my arm around her waist.

She stood on her toes and puckered her lips as she

waited for a kiss from me. I obliged and left a chaste kiss on her plump lips.

"You're just in time. My mother called me an hour or so ago to invite us for dinner. I was thinking about telling her and Luc about our extra addition tonight. I know it's still early, but I really want to tell her."

"Because you can't keep a secret," Nina joked at my character flaw. Secrets were hard for me to keep hold of and I was not the person to be trusted with one, especially a good secret like ours.

"Besides that, I think she should know. She's been so stressed with my sister, it will be something positive for her to look forward to," I explained to my gorgeous girlfriend who peered up at me through her long eyelashes.

Nina nodded in agreement as I kept her pulled close to me. I loved the feel of her and the way the curves of her body seemed to fit into my arms perfectly. Waking up every morning with her body against mine was what kept me going. I couldn't wait until I could feel the thuds of our baby kicking in her belly.

"Did you get a good workout?"

"As good as I can. I can't fucking *wait* to get this cast off," I grunted in frustration at the cast that covered nearly my entire arm. Once it came off, I'd have to go to physical therapy to rebuild my strength.

"The time will come," she reminded me as she did every time I complained about my situation. She had this way of forcing me out of my negativity and into a positive mindset. For someone who'd fought so much in her life, I was amazed at the positivity she was able to keep and spread. Without her, I didn't know how I'd survive.

MY MOM PULLED Nina in for a tight hug as soon as we arrived. She was looking a little worse for wear as of late. The bags under my mom's eyes were dark and sunken and streaks of gray were prominent throughout her normally dyed blonde hair. Exhaustion was taking its toll.

"It's so good to see you," she cheered as she pulled Nina along with her into the house.

"Uncle Marc," I heard the small, excited voice of my niece before I saw her bounding from the living room couch. She leaped onto me as soon as she reached me, and I picked her up with my good arm.

"Ma petite lapin," I cooed to the small girl whom I hadn't seen in weeks.

"Did you bring me a present?" Najah asked with a beaming smile and big doughy eyes. I chuckled for a moment and thought of how good it would feel to come home to my own little one jumping into my arms when I came home at the end of the day.

"Just me," I boasted proudly only to get a pout from her. "Où est ton frère?" I glanced around for her little brother who normally followed her every move.

"He's asleep," she told me with a little relief in her voice.

"Come to the kitchen," my mom's voice called from up the hall.

I hadn't realized she'd disappeared, taking Nina with her.

"Let's see what Mamy wants," I noted to my niece whom I kept in my arm as I strolled into the kitchen where Nina was seated with a glass of water at the table with Luc who was already nursing a beer, which was typical for him and my mother in the evening hours.

Mom produced a snack for Najah who wiggled from my arm and ran off to my mother to get her snack and sprinted back off toward the living room.

"So, Sophie's kids are here?" I questioned.

"Sophie is off doing God knows what and Basir had to work. Somebody had to take the kids," Mom argued.

"No, I understand," I agreed.

I settled at the table next to Nina and accepted a beer from my mom who poured it and placed it on the table in front of me. She took her own seat next to Luc and frowned as she looked me over.

"I don't like seeing you injured. I knew one day you would get hurt," she fussed as she shook her head. Mom hated I was still fighting but it'd given me purpose, at least until Nina. "Will you quit after this? Please tell me you will."

"I'm not planning on it," I informed her, which was the truth.

I wasn't going to let some injury keep me from doing what I loved. Hell, I needed to provide more than ever, I was starting a family. Nina would have to stop dancing eventually to finish off her pregnancy and while she healed. It was my time to step up and be the man of my home and provide for her and our child.

"I don't understand why you'd keep doing it. You're hurting your body," she pointed out, clearly upset as she slapped her hand on the table and her voice cracked.

"I need to provide, Mama," I told her sternly before I relaxed for a moment and took her hand into mine. "This might be a good time to break the tension with happy news."

"Happy news?" Her blue eyes now brightening up with intrigue.

Turning to Nina, I gave her a grin and she nodded at me, placing a hand on my shoulder. I'd won a shit ton of championships and remained undefeated but what I was about to say out loud for the first time was my honest to God pride and joy. This trumped all my achievements as a fighter, easily.

"Nina and I are expecting a baby," I said calmly to my mother's widening eyes followed by a loud and excited scream as she threw her arms around me and squeezed me tight.

"A baby?" She placed my head between her hands and I nodded in confirmation. She was suddenly ripping away from me and jolting from her chair. She ran directly to Nina and squeezed her just as tight as she'd done me. "I'm so happy. Congratulations, Nina and Marc. This is lovely."

"Thank you," Nina said sweetly as she hugged my mom back.

"That's great news, Gefeliciteerd!" Luc also cheered as he raised his beer to us.

"I'm over the moon," My mother stood in pure awe before she grabbed me again and kissed my cheek. "When are you due?"

"July," Nina answered her.

"And I bet your family is just as thrilled," Mom noted.

"If her family only knew," I snapped at the frustration that built in me. "Hell, if they only knew about us."

"Wait, your family doesn't know about you two?" Luc asked as he leaned in, intrigued.

"No," Nina answered plainly as she glared at me. She was clearly upset at me for bringing it up, but it bugged the fuck out of me. She didn't have to reveal the pregnancy right away, but she could at least be upfront about us seeing each other. Hell, we were practically living together.

"She's ashamed of me I guess," I said with a careless shrug.

"Marc," Nina hissed. I'd angered her, but I should and was the angry one. I was this sinful secret to her.

Loud pounds at the front door kept me from responding. Everyone at the table glanced at one another as the pounding continued. Najah jolted into the kitchen and under the table in fear, her small body trembled.

"Mama, laat me binnen!" My sister's voice screeched from outside.

"Mama?" Najah questioned as her head popped from under the table and peered out down the hall and in the direction of her mother's voice as she continued to rap at the door and scream for my mother to let her in.

"She's drunk," my mother whispered as she shook her head.

"I'll take care of it," I told her with a hand on her shoulder.

Standing, I left the kitchen behind and up the hallway toward the front door. The loud pounds of my sister continued until I opened the door and there she stood. Sophie looked worse for wear. Her clothes were hanging off her, her eyes bloodshot, and her dark hair pulled back in a ponytail that hadn't been redone in days. My father's abuse had led to her abusing herself.

"Big Brother," she blurted as she threw her arms around me. I could smell the stench of the alcohol practically pouring through her pores.

"Sophie," I mentioned as I looked her over once more. I'd seen her bad but never this bad. She clearly hadn't changed her clothes in days and had been out drinking and gambling for a long time. "How are you?"

"I'm so good," she slurred as she stumbled past and into the house. "I'm here to get the kids. Basir said they were here."

"No, you aren't," I concluded easily as I stepped in

front of her to block her from going any closer to the kitchen.

"Marc, stop. Let me get the kids," she argued as she tried her hardest to move me out of her way. I wouldn't let her take a single step forward, not the way she was, wasted out of her brains.

"Sophie, you're drunk. I'm not letting you take them until you're sober. I'll get you a taxi home, you can sober up, and come back tomorrow," I told her as calmly as possible.

"Fuck off!" she shot. "You can't tell me what I can and cannot do with *my* children." She swung at me, but I caught her wrist easily in my hand and held onto it.

"Calm down, let's get you home and you can get the kids tomorrow. You don't want them seeing you like this." I tried my damnedest to stay as calm as possible. I didn't want Najah alarmed nor have Kamil woken up with her racket.

With a deep breath, I took a step forward in hopes she would take a step back. I kept my cool as she still tried to struggle with me but was losing that battle even with a broken arm. Sophie peered up at me and behind her dull blue eyes, I saw the little girl our dad would beat relentlessly. She was begging for help.

"Zusje," I cooed to her as I kept our eye contact strong. After a moment, I could feel her fight diminishing and a tear slipped from her eye. "Come on, let me get you home. Tomorrow you can see the kids and then we're going to get you some help. Okay?"

"Okay," she nodded and pressed her face to my

shirt. Soft sobs erupted from her and I held her closely. "He's always in my head. I'm just trying to fight him off."

"Same here," I confirmed with her as I allowed her to cry and held her.

The door to the kitchen opened and I saw Nina's head pop out. She watched us for a moment before she carefully stepped up the hall toward Sophie and myself. Sophie glanced around me to see Nina.

"Wie is dat?" Sophie questioned.

"That's my girlfriend, Nina," I told my sister before turning to Nina. "I'm going to take her in a taxi home. I'll meet you back at my place, okay?"

"Okay, I'll see you." With a hand on my shoulder, Nina gave it a squeeze before I turned back to my sister who had a goofy smile on her face.

"I'll take Nina home, don't worry," Mom said from the kitchen door. I gave her a smile of thanks before I put my focus back on Sophie.

"Let's get you a taxi and get you home."

———

FLIPPING on the light in my sister's apartment, immediately I saw it was a mess. There were toys and clothes scattered all around. The kitchen sink was piled with dishes, and there was even a diaper on the floor next to the garbage can. The worst part was the stench that filled the air and burned the hairs inside my nose.

Stepping deeper into the living room, I shook my

head at the sight of beer and other alcohol bottles littering the coffee table along with baby bottles. Sophie had spiraled so deep I was honestly afraid there was no pulling her out of it.

I sighed as I noticed the television was no longer in its place. Sophie had likely sold it to gamble with. It took me back to when I came home from school one day to find our TV set was gone. Our father had taken it and sold it on the street to fuel his habit. He'd of course come home broke and drunk. When Sophie and I asked about the television, he'd laid into us and gave us one of those beatings that would stay with us forever.

"Let's get you to bed," I mentioned to Sophie who hung off my good arm. She was out of it and it was definitely time to get her to bed to sober up.

Leading her down the hall, I navigated around toys left discarded by the kids and into her small bedroom. The sheets were twisted, and blanket thrown off on the floor, but I could manage it. I helped her onto the bed and got her to lay down before I tossed the blanket over her as best I could with one arm.

"Sit with me," she requested.

I sat on the edge of the bed and placed a hand on her arm. I remembered the day my sister was born, and my grandmother took me to the hospital to meet the small baby girl. From that day, all I ever wanted to do was protect her as best I could. So many days I couldn't keep her from getting the brunt of Dad's beatings, but I tried.

When we didn't have enough food to eat, I'd purposely go without so that Sophie could get a proper helping. I took my role as big brother seriously and I still did. We only had each other when it came down to it and I sure as hell wouldn't let her suffer alone.

"Your girlfriend is pretty," she murmured as she lay with her eyes closed. "I'm happy for you, Big Brother."

"Thanks. I really need you to take this seriously and get yourself straight, for you, for Mom, and most importantly your kids," I made clear. Najah and Kamil needed their mother around. They needed both their parents around, but Sophie had to get herself together for that.

"I will. I know I need to get better," she told me.

"Good, now get some sleep, tomorrow starts your new life."

I waited until she was snoring, and I left her alone in her room. Beginning in the hall, I began to pick up toys and other objects on the floor until I arrived in the living room. Sophie would wake up to a clean apartment that was ready for healing. I only had one arm to work with, but I'd use it well and spend all night if I had to.

CHAPTER FOURTEEN

NINA

Marc's deep laughter filled the bedroom as we laid together. His hand over my bump and rubbing as kicks returned at his touch. Since our baby started kicking, this was how we spent most evenings in bed, with Marc loving the connection he was already building with the life inside me.

"Hey little fella," Marc chuckled at the latest kick to his hand. I shook my head and gave a mock pout in his direction.

"What if its not a boy. Could be a girl. There is a fifty-fifty chance," I reminded him as I tended to do whenever Marc tried to stake his claim that our baby was a boy. I really didn't care what we had. I just wanted a healthy, happy baby in the end. It sounded so cliché but after losing a baby once, I just wanted to have a perfectly happy baby to mother.

"I'm sorry. Garçon ou fille, I'm happy. You know

that." Marc rubbed my arm with is rough hand. My hairs stood on end and I shivered at his touch.

Marc leaned in and planted a kiss on my shoulder. Then another as he moved toward my neck. As gentle kisses rained over my skin, my breathing became deep and uneven before he planted a final kiss on my ear as his hand traveled over my bare thigh and under my night gown that was becoming shorter as my belly grew.

With fingers between my thickening thighs, Marc easily slipped his hand under the fabric of my panties and between my folds.

"Fuck, I love how wet you get," he growled in my ear as he began to stroke over my overly sensitive clit. I gasped sharply before a moan took over and my body shook under his touch.

Pregnancy had intensified everything and threw my sex drive into overdrive. Marc could barely touch me, and I was easily lusting and ready to rip my clothes off. It also didn't help that he'd discovered the magic of wearing sweatpants around me, which I felt like he was doing more often.

"Oh. My. God," I panted as he drove me toward an orgasm easily as my body naturally rocked into his hand. "Keep going," I begged as my fingers gripped onto his shirt so hard my knuckles were turning white.

"Let it go, baby," Marc murmured to me as I started to orgasm. I tremored as my hormones flung me through euphoria at only this man's delicious touch.

As I came down, Marc removed his hand and held it

up. It glistened with my release. I shyly looked down. I was still learning to enjoy sex without shame. It wasn't shameful, but oddly beautiful.

"Looks like you made a mess," Marc observed before bringing his hand to his mouth and licking his fingers. I could have come again at the sight of him licking my juices. "C'est bonne."

"Fuck me," I gasped as I tried to control myself. I needed him more and the buzzing that filled my body from between my legs wouldn't stop without having him.

Marc laughed.

"What's so funny?" I grunted in frustration.

"It's funny seeing you, this pure woman, demanding to be fucked like some crazed animal," he chuckled.

"I am a crazed animal thanks to pregnancy. Please, Marc. I need you," I whined before I slipped my hand in my panties. "Or I'll take care of it myself."

Marc snatched my hand out of my underwear and held it with the other over my head, his body now on top of mine pinning me down, but not hard enough to hurt me or the baby.

"No, you won't," he growled. "My Belgian Beast is going to take care of that." Easily, he slid his sweatpants lower, exposing the curly hairs at the end of his V that lay just above the main event. I groaned as he stopped before showing me what I wanted. He chuckled lightly before bending and kissing my lips. "I'm going to get off you. I need you to take off your gown and panties and get on your knees. Okay?"

I nodded eagerly and bit down on my bottom lip.

The moment Marc allowed me free, I sat up, and pulled my gown over my head exposing my naked torso with my nipples pointed and hard. I next worked on my panties and pulled them down my legs before I tossed them in Marc's direction. He easily caught them and pressed them to his face.

"Mmm," he murmured before tossing them to the side and ripping his sweatpants down all the way. I gaped at him as I did every single time. He was hard to not gape at with his muscular body, and rock-hard dick that bounced ready to be inside me. He gave me a stern look as he motioned for me to follow his final instruction and turn over.

Doing as I'd been told, I got on my hands and knees. I could feel Marc join me on the bed with the movement of the mattress. He came up behind me, his hands settling on my ass that he apparently couldn't get enough of. Sensing the vixen inside, I wiggled my ass a little before he landed a smack over my skin.

"You're being a little tease this evening, aren't you?" his deep voice questioned from behind me.

"Maybe," I coyly answered before gasping at his hands gripping my sides and his dick pressing into me quicker than I'd anticipated. "Marc," I moaned as our bodies began slapping together.

Marc rode into me, deeper and harder with each thrust. I cried out at the feel of him filling me. Our connection was so strong that it alone rocked me to my core. I tried to control my breathing, but it was impossible as Marc looped a hand around and began to stroke my clit.

Easily, I came again. I was barely able to breath as his own grunts and growls filled the air, and his deep hard thrusts became shorter as he spilled into me.

As Marc came out of me, I found myself laying on my back working to catch my breath. Marc wrapped his arms around me and pulled the blanket over our sweaty bodies. I snuggled in deep as I began to trace one of his tattoos with the tip of my finger.

"I discover a new detail every single time," I mentioned as I paused over the delicately etched ink on his skin.

"Same," Marc murmured into my hair. "I didn't know you liked to get spanked. I'll have to remember that."

"Oh, shut up," I slapped his chest with my hand. As much as I loved having sex, talking about it was still embarrassing.

"My sweet innocent one," Marc commented with a hint of irony. "The mother of my child. I can't wait to find out what we're having. My little one." He ran a hand over my belly and of course our baby was once again kicking up a storm.

"We need to think of names. I want something different but traditional, at least one of his or her names has to be a good Muslim name," I mentioned. It was something important to me. My faith meant a lot to myself and my family.

"Are we raising our child Muslim?" Marc slightly

sat up and looked at me. Sometimes I couldn't tell what he was thinking, and it was hard to know if his look was good or bad.

"I'd like to. It means a lot to me to have my child grow with faith," I insisted as I also sat up.

"Nina, I don't know about that. I'd like our baby to know about your faith and my sad lack of but I don't know if we should raise him or her to have a specific faith," Marc argued as he was not sitting straight up and arguing his case to me.

I frowned. My entire life, my faith in Islam had been a cornerstone for my family. I couldn't imagine my life without. Yes, I didn't always agree and didn't always followed bit it still had a place in my heart.

"Please, this is one thing that means so much to me."

"But why? What's so important about it that it is a *must*? I don't want our child to be outcasted, treated differently, or excluded based on the fact that they have a specific faith. You know, first-hand, that Belgium isn't exactly welcoming recently." Marc made a point, but it infuriated me. My baby shouldn't have to live in a world that didn't treat them the same as others just because they were a follower of Islam and I hated that Marc made the case against using that example.

I gave a frustrated grunt and swung the blanket off me. I stormed into the bathroom and turned on the shower. I had to calm myself down. Marc had struck something in me. I stepped into the water the moment it warmed and allowed it to trickle over my skin.

Closing my eyes, I breathed steadily in and out

before a hand rested on my shoulder and I jumped at Marc who had joined me. He pulled me in close and settled his head on my shoulder.

"I'm sorry, love. I am. I know it's important to you, but I really don't want to make those decisions for our baby. I don't feel like it is our place. Look at our situation, you're forced into hiding us and our baby because of your faith and your family's dedication to it. I'd be afraid of our child facing those same consequences for going off the chosen path. Maybe we could agree to let him or her pick that path. We can introduce it but not make it law," Marc reasoned to me.

I turned to him and nodded as I placed my arms around his neck.

"I can agree to that," I said softly. It wasn't a difficult decision. Our child would participate in family events and learn about the faith, but we wouldn't force it. I didn't want my child like me, afraid to step into happiness. "I just want our baby to be happy in the end and that's all that matters to me."

"Me too," Marc agreed. "I think he will be."

"Or maybe a she," I argued to Marc laughing at me.

"Or maybe a she." He planted a kiss on the tip of my nose. "I love how we can easily work things out."

"Me too," I said before making the point, "most of the time."

———

FROM THE MOMENT my bump popped, my mission

was to hide it in every way possible. At five months along, my family was still left in the dark. I still saw them almost every Friday as if nothing was different in my life, but it was. I was waiting for the birth of my child in secret. Every moment I stressed about how they'd feel or react. I was afraid of them knowing.

Every week, I watched my sister-in-law grow and my mother dote over the child still growing inside of her. I hated I couldn't have the same and with each visit, I grew jealous of the attention she received when I was also giving the gift of life.

Luckily, the conversations with my family were no longer revolved around how I was too skinny. My mother was proud of my weight gain and how my face was clearly filling out and I wasn't a twig anymore.

Getting off the metro, I tried to walk as normal as possible, but I was beginning to develop a waddle in my step. Leaving the metro station, I waddled toward the entrance of the university hospital I was being seen at throughout my pregnancy. I had an appointment and Marc was supposed to meet me at the hospital once he finished his physical therapy session as it was at the same hospital.

As soon as I stepped inside the automatic doors, arms came around my waist and a kiss planted on my lips. I didn't have to see him but only smell his scent and take in the feel of his strong arms to know it was the love of my life.

"How was class?" Marc laced our fingers and we began toward the check-in and registration area.

"Good. There is so much to do still before they perform on Saturday," I told him.

It was time for the Dance Conservatory's big Winter Showcase and all my girls, and one boy, would be performing over the weekend. My schedule was full as we added extra rehearsals and costume fittings into the schedule to prepare. I was stretching myself, but I knew it would all be worth it in the end for my students to show their skills.

"Don't overdo it," Marc nudged me.

"I'll be fine," I told him as we approached the registration screen and I did what I had to do, check-in for my appointment. This was my life every February but being pregnant did make all the running around much tougher.

With my hand in his, we strolled through the large hospital to the Obstetrics and Gynecology department. Today was the most exciting appointment of all as we were prepared to learn the sex of our baby. We'd spent the last few nights in bed thinking up names for a boy or a girl and imagining our future with them in our lives.

"How are you feeling in there today, mon Chouchou?" Marc asked my belly as we took a seat in the waiting room and he placed his hand over my rounded bump. As usual, whenever Marc touched my belly, the baby would instantly kick back. "Somebody's excited for us to see you."

"Nina Sangare," my name was called, and I looked up to see my blonde doctor standing in the doorway to the exam room. Marc stood with me and placed his hand gently on the small of my back as we followed my doctor into the examination room. "Comment allez vous?" She closed the door.

"Fatigué," I answered with a huff. Pregnancy was exhausting and it didn't help I was doing what I could to keep my pregnancy quiet. That in and of itself was extremely tiring.

"That's normal unless you're feeling dizzy or overly exhausted. Try to keep cool and drink lots of fluids," she reminded sweetly as she motioned for me to head over to the table next to the ultrasound machine. "Let's see this baby."

Getting on the table, I lifted my sweater to reveal my rounded and protruding stomach. My belly button was beginning to poke outward and I could see the motion of the baby while feeling it inside me.

"Active today?" The doctor sat down on the stool with the machine and Marc sat on the other side of me taking my hand into his and squeezing it tight.

"Every day," I commented as I thought of the constant bumps and kicks I'd receive nearly all day, every day from my little secret.

As the doctor squeezed the gel onto my stomach, I shivered at how cold it was and glanced over to Marc who was in awe of everything as he was at every appointment. His eyes were wide and peering all over the place before settling on my eyes and a smile came to his lips. I smiled back before he bent over to me and gave me a chaste kiss.

Starting the ultrasound, I could see what the doctor saw on the screen above my head. She showed us the feet, legs, heart, arms, fingers, and little face before we finally got to what we'd been waiting for. My heart pounded in anticipation.

"Are you ready to find out the sex?" My doctor asked us excitedly.

"Oui, oui," I cheered as I tried to not hold my breath.

"It looks like a boy."

I immediately glanced over to Marc who was beaming with joy. When we'd lay in bed talking about our future, he always talked about our son. His dream was coming true.

"Un garçon," he gushed before he grabbed both sides of my face and kissed me hard. "Bonjour, Axel."

It was the name we'd settled on together for a boy. After weeks of back and forth we'd narrowed it down to a handful of names for each sex until we'd come up with one name for each. Our baby boy would be Axel Mohamed Vandenberghe.

Leaving the appointment, Marc and I gushed over the ultrasound photos we'd received. I couldn't believe that every day, week, and month was moving so incredibly fast. It wouldn't be long before I had a baby boy in my arms.

"My mom is going to scream," Marc noted as we strolled into the Metro station together, fingers intertwined. I thought of Charlotte and how every time I saw her, she would gush about how thrilled she was for Marc to become a father. "What about your mom?"

"Please, Marc," I murmured, not wanting to go into it. I still hadn't thought of how I'd tell my family. I knew I'd tell my mother first, she was the least of my worries, at least I hoped.

Marc let out an annoyed huff as he generally did when I tried to get away from the conversation. We scanned our tickets and went through the gates of the station and began toward the platform.

"I don't see why you're so fucking ashamed of the fact that you're having my child," Marc argued. It wasn't that I was ashamed of having his child. I knew how my family would take it and I wasn't ready for the drama that would ensue. Plus, I knew my parents could never look at me the same way again.

"I'm not ashamed," I concluded. "I just know it will be a mess. I know I can't avoid it for too much longer but I'm not ready."

"What's the worst that can happen?" He asked as we waited on the platform for our train.

"For starters, my brother will try to kill you, literally," I noted knowing exactly how it would go down. "My mother will be an emotional wreck, and my dad…" My voice trailed off before I swallowed down the lump in my throat. "I don't want to be the reason he has another heart attack."

"Ma petite danseuse," Marc cooed with an arm around my shoulder as he bent to me and kissed my cheek. "Don't think that way."

"It's hard not to." I wiped away my tears. I was constantly an emotional wreck. I was already emotional before pregnancy but with child everything made my cry easily.

"At the end of the day, we have each other. We make our family complete."

"We do." Peering into Marc's bright blue eyes, I saw our future together. It would be us and our baby boy, but the thought of losing my family's love and support did scare me. I already lived on the edge of not being fully accepted.

Marc rubbed my arm before he took my hand into his while his other one reached into his pocket.

"I wanted to wait until dinner tonight. I had this huge plan. Dinner at the Grand Place, there's even a musician waiting but fuck that. It's not me anyway. I'm a simple guy and it makes more since to do this simply, the only way I really know how." I was so confused to what he was going on about. "Ever since I picked this up this afternoon, I can't wait. You know me and secrets," he joked with a sloppy grin before he dropped to one knee in the middle of the metro station. "Nina, I love you. I love our son, and I love the life we're building together. You literally dropped into my life from heaven. This quiet and graceful dancer changed everything and I'm never going back to how my life was before. Nina Sangare, will you marry me?"

From his pocket, Marc produced a simple yet perfect ring. The silver band held a single princess cut diamond. I couldn't believe my eyes or my ears, but only one thing was for sure: I wanted to be with him forever.

"Oui! Oui! Oui!" I screamed over and over as Marc slipped the ring onto my finger before standing and pulled me in for a deep kiss that took my senses away.

I hadn't noticed the small crowd of people that gathered in the station as Marc was proposing. They all cheered and shouted their congratulations. It wasn't the most romantic spot, the middle of the metro station, but it was absolutely perfect, exactly how Marc described himself, it was *simply* perfect.

I WAS POWERING through my day. I'd been all over Brussels in only a matter of hours from the conservatory for rehearsals and costume alterations, to the venue of the show, and back home to change my clothes before I was quickly off to my parent's home as usual for a Friday.

Staying home and climbing into bed would have been the better idea with how run down I felt. My entire body was physically exhausted, and I hurt from head to toe. Ignoring the pain and my exhaustion, I rang the bell at my parent's home and hugged my oversized sweater around my body.

I knew if I stayed home, Mom would call asking a million questions, and if I told her I wasn't feeling well, she would be at my house cooking me food there. It wasn't worth all the trouble and I'd rather bite the bullet and get it over with.

"Ma petite!" Dad cheered as he opened the door. He beamed from ear to ear as he pulled me in for a hug. "Nina est arrivé!" he announced as we entered the house. "Ça va? Ma petite?"

"Ça va, et vous?" I asked as we strolled into the living room where Suzanna sat rubbing her oversized belly and watching television with her other children who were all lost in the show.

"Ça va," Dad answered as he parked himself in his armchair as usual.

"Bonjour à tous," I greeted everyone, patting the children on their heads and kissing Suzanna on the cheek as usual.

"How much are you eating? I swear you gain more weight each time I see you," Suzanna commented. I took a deep breath and didn't respond to my sister-in-law, who never had anything nice to say.

Leaving the living room, and Suzanna's constantly negative energy, I went off to find my mom who was hard at work in the kitchen with my grandmother. The smell of a lot of different food still made me nauseous but I wasn't jogging off to the bathroom to vomit as I did in the beginning.

"Nina, you look tired," Mom commented.

"I'm fine, Maman," I countered before I gave my grandmother a kiss on the cheek. "Bonjour Mamy."

"My beautiful. Look at that round face, you remind me of when your mother was pregnant with those round cheeks," My grandma commented as she reached up and pinched my cheek. I offered a weak smile at her comment. Maybe I could tell them tonight … or not.

Moments later, there were more people entering the kitchen. My aunt and uncle came in along with Ayo's sister, Arjana, and her children. There was loud chatter as my brother also arrived from a late day at work.

I snuck out of the madness and back into the living room where Ayo sat on the couch texting. He'd dyed the tips of his hair blond and had gotten a nose ring. When the nose ring first appeared, my aunt lost her shit but Ayo being Ayo, ignored the drama and went about his business.

Dad got out of his chair and left us with Suzanna and my brother's children.

"Cousine!" He cheered as he saw me.

I took my usual seat with him on the loveseat opposite Suzanna and her pack of children.

"How are you feeling?"

"I'm tired but okay," I told him as I resisted the urge to rub my hand over my belly at Axel's relentless kicks. I think he smelled his grandmother's cooking and was excited for all the eating we'd do.

Leaning in closer, Ayo kept his voice low to keep Suzanna from eavesdropping on our conversation. She was known to not just be nosey but to be a snitch.

"Did you find out?" he asked me anxiously.

"On Tuesday," I informed him as I tried to keep

from grinning so hard, but it was difficult when I wanted to scream it from the rooftops the way Marc wanted to. "It's a boy."

"A boy," he tried to whisper his scream before he threw his arms around me and hugged me tightly. "Oh cousin, I'm so happy for you. I know Marc is excited."

"Marc is more than excited. We're supposed to go look at houses down in Hainaut this weekend," I informed my cousin.

"And I'm going to decorate," he declared instantly.

"Decorate what?" The joy in the air was met with the voice of my sister-in-law who enjoyed injecting herself into business that wasn't hers to be in.

"I'm looking at apartments," I plainly stated.

"Nice," she simply commented before she stood and left the room.

Glancing over to Ayo, he rolled his eyes and I shook my head. We were used to Suzanna and her constantly wanting to be involved in other's business but the moment someone commented on her life it was a problem.

"Nina, Suzanna says you're moving?" Mom called from the other room.

"Bitch," Ayo muttered under his breath before I stood with Ayo behind me.

After my first step, I paused for a moment in place as I suddenly felt a wave of dizziness come over me. Earlier in the day I'd felt the same but after taking a deep breath, it'd gone away. Just as earlier my dizzy spell began to end, and I continued into the kitchen where the rest of the family was gathered.

"Nina says she's looking at apartments," Suzanna told my aunt who stood over a bowl rolling balls of Foutou Banane, which was a favorite of mine as a kid and Ayo's mom made the best.

"Out of Jette?" Dad asked.

"Yes," I answered as I my dizzy spell returned with much more intensity than before.

Suddenly I felt as if I wanted to vomit as well and my skin prickled with sweat. I was burning from the inside out. My vision began to blur and though people were speaking to me, I could barely make out what they were saying. My mom approached me. I could just make out her face, but her voice wasn't translating. Nothing made sense and my head was spinning with the room before it all went black.

CHAPTER FIFTEEN

MARC

My heart didn't stop beating a million times a minute from the moment Ayo called me. I didn't have time to think about anything else but getting to Nina as soon as possible. The ride through Brussels was a blur. I barely remembered the blue lights of the Madou Tunnel as I whipped through it fast as lightning on my motorcycle.

Presently, there were no such things as traffic rules in my book and I'd likely racked up quite a few tickets from the speed cameras placed around the city. My priority was Nina and my son.

Arriving in Halle, the last time I'd been to this hospital was when I'd come to see Nina when her father had his heart attack. I parked my bike at the entrance and jogged inside ripping my helmet off as I approached the glass window of the emergency room receptionist.

"Hoe kan ik u helpen?" The woman behind the glass asked what she could help me with.

"Nina Sangare, she was brought here. Can I see her?" I asked frantically before I heard my name called from behind me.

I sharply turned to see Ayo sitting with a group of people I recognized from photos. Nina's family sat huddled together in the waiting room. They all stared at me like I had two heads as I approached them.

"How is she?" I asked them instantly wanting to know her current condition. All I knew was that she fainted at her parent's house and they called the ambulance.

"She's awake and alert," Ayo informed me which already calmed my heartbeat from the frantic thumping that had filled my chest. "She passed out from exhaustion and dehydration. They are giving her fluids and monitoring her and the baby."

"And the baby is good?" I inquired.

"As far as they can tell, but we don't have too much information. Her mom is with her," he told me with a long face. "I'm sorry but I had to tell them. She suddenly fainted and I knew we had to get her to a hospital."

"I understand and thanks for it." I patted Ayo on the shoulder in appreciation. "I want to see her," I demanded wanting to be with Nina and the knowledge that our son was completely fine.

"And who are you?" A deep voice asserted from behind Ayo. A tall man stood and moved him from the path that separated us. He wasn't as tall as me but had some height on him. I knew from photos he was Nina's older brother, Jaheem.

I puffed out my chest and stood tall at his already defensive stance.

He stepped closer and we were toe to toe.

"I'm Marc," I answered his question.

"Okay, Marc. What do you want with my sister?" He snarled and looked me over from head to toe and back.

"First, I'm her fiancé. Second, I'm her baby's father," I stated plainly and easily.

"Oh, Allah," gasped one of the women seated. Her hand was over her mouth and her eyes filled with shock. "Fiancé?" She looked around at the other women in the group who were equally shocked.

"You did this to my daughter?" Growled another voice. A man I knew was Nina's father stood, his eyes wild with anger as he approached.

He and her brother both stood trying to intimidate me which wasn't going to happen. I would do what I had to. My only concern was Nina and Axel's wellbeing. I wouldn't let them stand in my way.

"Did what?" I asked wondering what he meant. I hadn't done anything wrong to Nina. I only loved her and was prepared to do it forever.

"Raped my sister," he growled before spitting at the ground. "Dégueulasse, sale blanc."

I tried my hardest to hold my composure as her brother insulted me and insinuated that I had taken advantage of Nina. I wouldn't let him put that on me. Never. He was fucking with the wrong man.

"I did *not* rape her," I hissed as I got my face directly in his. "Don't you fucking dare let me hear you say that again."

"Rapist," he spat with a smirk on his lips, pleased he was egging me on.

"Arrêtez!" I heard Ayo's voice, but I couldn't even focus on him.

With all my might I shoved Jaheem as hard as I could. Gasps came from the family. He stumbled back and fell to the floor, his eyes wild as he jumped back up, his adrenaline likely rushing through him as mine did with me.

"I'll fucking kill you. You defiled my sister!" He charged at me, but I easily pulled him into a headlock before slamming his body to the ground.

"I dare you to fucking try," I spat before I made a beeline to the counter where the woman I'd spoken to only moments before sat in awe of what she'd witnessed. "I'm Nina Sangare's fiancé and the child's father, I want to see her *now*."

"I will see what I can do. Een moment." She quickly picked up the phone and began to speak rapidly to the person on the other end. "Someone will meet you at the door and escort you."

"He will not go near my daughter," Nina's father growled from the waiting room, but I ignored him and strolled to the electric door that was opening for me.

A male nurse stood, and I could tell by his jittery

body language that he was apprehensive as his eyes scanned the waiting room where Nina's family was in hysterics.

Following the nurse, the doors behind us automatically closed and the noise of the family disappeared. I could only hear machines and low chatting at this point as we strolled down a hall. We stopped at a room and the nurse slid the door open. I saw Nina and I forgot everything from before. I only saw her and rushed to her side where she lay in the hospital bed with her mother sitting on the other side of the room.

"Who are you?" Her mother shot instantly as I held Nina's hand and squeezed it.

"He's the father," Nina answered quietly as she peered up at me.

Her mother's hands went over her mouth and not a single word came from her mouth as she watched us.

Sitting on the edge of the bed, I stroked Nina's cheek. Her dark skin was gray, and she was clammy. Her sick look reminded me of her early pregnancy when she was constantly nauseated and throwing up.

"How are you feeling?" I asked as I continued to stroke her cheek with my thumb.

"Better," she answered as she leaned into my hand.

"And Axel?" I asked placing my other hand on her stomach and instantly I smiled as I felt our baby boy kicking away as usual. It set my mind at a little more ease knowing that Nina was stable, and Axel didn't seem affected at all.

"He's good. They want to move me to labor and

delivery to observe me overnight, but we're both good," Nina explained before I bent to her and kissed her gently. "I love you."

"I love you."

"How could you do this, Nina?" Her mother's voice cut through the air and I felt Nina instantly tense. "Did you not use your brain?"

"Maman, please," Nina begged.

"You know better than that. Think of the shame you've already brought on our family and now this. I'm so disappointed." Nina's mother began to cry and in only moments Nina was sobbing in my arms.

I knew this moment was what she was trying to avoid. It was intense from the waiting room to the triage. Nina didn't need it, what she needed was to be loved unconditionally. I loved her with no conditions and if I was all she would have left at the end of this, so be it. They were going to lose out on an amazing woman and eventually a great little boy.

"Please, Madame, I don't want her upset right now," I insisted as I faced her mother for the first time.

"I need to go. I can barely even look at you." Suddenly her mother stood and left the room without a look back.

Nina sobbed harder as she gripped onto me and pressed her face onto my chest. Her family was turning their backs to her when she needed them the most.

"I knew this would happen," she cried as she laid back onto her pillow and wiped her tears that continued to fall.

"My brother and dad will lose their shit," she said as she shook her head.

"They already did," I reluctantly told her.

"What happened?"

"You don't want to know right now. Right now, you need to rest up for you and for Axel. He needs his mama well, okay?"

Nina nodded and gripped onto my hand tightly. We had each other and that's what mattered most.

———

A KNOCK on the edge of the door brought me out of my light sleep. Nina had been moved during the night to the maternity ward where she was under observation. I never left her side and slept in a chair in the corner.

Opening my eyes, I expected another nurse or midwife to be coming in to check Nina's vitals as they did like clockwork but instead it was my mother who gave a weak smile and carried a potted plant into the room.

Nina was fast asleep after her emotional night and being poked and prodded by doctors and nurses. She needed the rest more than anything since exhaustion is what landed her in the hospital in the first place. She was upset that she'd miss the performance of her students, but she knew she'd run herself too much and it was time for her to take a step back from balancing so many responsibilities. At least she no longer had the work of hiding her pregnancy.

"Goedemorgen," My mom greeted in a whisper as she crossed the room to me and pulled me into a hug. "How is she and the baby?"

"They're both good," I told her as I kept my voice quiet to allow Nina to get her much needed rest. "The baby is being monitored and he's been constantly active which is good. Nina is still tired and this morning the doctor mentioned keeping her another day."

"I'm happy everything is good. She was with her family when she collapsed, right?" Mom asked.

I sighed.

"That bad?"

"It was a mess. Her brother tried to make claims I raped her, and he attacked me in the waiting room. Her dad was yelling, and her mom just walked out on her. Nina said this would happen, but I really didn't think it would be this bad. I hate that they are putting her through this. It happened, it's time to move on and celebrate our son's life," I expressed as I felt incredibly sad for Nina whom I glanced over to as she continued to lightly snore.

"She has us. She's family no matter what," My mom boasted. She'd accepted Nina from the first moment without batting an eye. "Sophie sent the plant."

"I'll text her later to thank her."

My sister had gone into a program to deal with her addictions. She'd been sober the last four months and gambling was a thing of the past. She'd made the decision to go to cosmetology school and worked at a daycare during the day. Things were looking up including she and Basir had gotten married and moved into a place near my mom.

"Do you think her family will ever come around?" Mom asked the million-dollar question.

"I have no idea. I'm hoping that her mom at least does." I hoped everyone came around and would accept us the way my family had. Nina didn't deserve to be shunned by her family. It might not be the exact relationship they saw her having but at least it was a loving one and the best part was our love had created a life.

A soft squeal and yawn from the bed alerted me to Nina who was coming out of her deep sleep. Her eyes fluttered open and glanced around for a moment until they landed on me and my mom who sat in the corner. I stood and sat on the edge of the bed taking her hand into mine.

"You slept really good for the last couple of hours," I told her as I stroked her hand gently.

Nina simply yawned as my mom also approached. Nina smiled up at her as she worked to sit up in bed.

"Bonjour, Nina," my mom greeted her cheerfully. "I just came to check on you and little Axel. Sophie also sent a plant."

"Thank you so much," Nina beamed at the thoughtfulness of my mom and sister. "It means a lot to me. It really does." I leaned over and kissed Nina on the forehead. "Did you finally get some sleep too?"

"A little," I told her as I stroked her smooth cheek.

There was another knock at the door, and we all turned expecting hospital staff when instead there were two men, and one woman dressed in blue, police. They all entered the room and approached the three of us.

"Is there a problem?" I immediately asked in Dutch wondering what the hell was going on.

"Goedemorgen, we received a complaint from a Mohamed Sangare. Do you know him?" one of the policemen asked.

"I do," I answered.

"He's my father," Nina added sitting up a little more.

"Mr. Sangare claims that a Marc Vandenberghe—"

"Me," I asserted.

"He's claiming that you, Mr. Vandenberghe, raped his daughter, Nina Sangare and yesterday in the hospital lobby physically attacked his son. We will need to speak with Ms. Sangare, alone." I stared at the policeman wildly as I couldn't believe a word that came out of his mouth. Nina's parents were trying to sabotage my name and assassinate my character with lies.

"I never raped her," I growled angrily as I stood up straight.

"He didn't," Nina insisted along with me. "This is crazy. Marc is my fiancé. We're having a baby. Did they really file a complaint?"

"They did and we must speak with you alone," the policewoman interjected.

Nina's eyes were wide as she glanced at me. She was

filled with a raw hurt I didn't think she could ever come back from and she might never forgive her parents for what they'd done.

"That's fine," Nina swallowed.

"I'll be right outside, okay, mon chéri?" I rubbed Nina's hand once more before I let it go.

"Okay," she squeaked as reality hit her and tears began to streak down her face.

I wanted to stay with her and hold her tight but one of the policemen had already taken ahold of my arm and was pulling me toward the door. I yanked my arm away.

"If I'm not being arrested or charged with something don't manhandle me like a criminal," I sneered in his direction. I easily towered the man who gave me a nod and motioned for me to exit the room civilly with the other officer following while the female stayed with Nina.

"What is all this about?" My mother inquired as she followed myself and the police officers into the hall. "My son did not rape her. They are getting married."

"Ma'am, alsjeblieft. We only have a few questions for your son," the second male officer insisted before he turned from my mom back to me as I stood against the wall opposite Nina's room. My eyes stayed staring through the small glass window at Nina who was speaking to the female officer. "Mr. Vandenberghe, how do you know Nina Sangare?"

"I'm her fiancé. We met in September and have been together since. Her parents are lying because they don't want us together," I explained as I tried to remain calm but it was pretty fucking hard when being accused of rape.

"And you are the baby's father?" The second officer inquired.

"I am. Her family didn't know about me, nor the baby, until yesterday when she fainted while with them and she was rushed here by ambulance. They didn't take any of the news well. I'm not quite the type of guy they want her with." I shrugged as I told them the absolute fucking truth.

"What do you do for a living Mr. Vandenberghe?" The shorter of the policemen asked as he eyed me. I'd come to the hospital directly from the gym. I was in my usual sweatpants and a tank top.

"I'm a Mixed Martial Arts fighter."

"Do you know that guy, the Belgian Beast?" The second, taller officer asked with excitement.

I laughed. "I am the Belgian Beast."

The officer gaped at me until the door to Nina's room opened and the female officer exited the room and stepped toward us.

"Can I go back to my fiancé now?" I asked anxiously as I itched to be back at her side. She gave me a nod and I bolted from the wall and back into Nina's room where she sat on the bed with the most distraught look on her face.

"I'm so sorry," she said in her soft voice as I sat on the edge of her bed and took her hand back into mine. "I didn't think they would do something like that. For them to make that accusation is beyond me. I'm so sorry, baby."

"It's fine and we'll be fine."

"Just a moment, what happened with Ms. Sangare's brother?" the female officer interrogated as she reentered the room with her follow officers and my mom behind.

"He did get in my personal space, I shoved him away before he attacked me. I simply defended myself," I stated matter-of-factly. "I'm sure you can view the surveillance footage from downstairs. If anything, *I* should be the one pressing charges, but I won't do that. He is my fiancée's brother after all, and I understand he was emotional."

"Oh my God," Nina gasped with a hand over her mouth. "He didn't?"

"He said he was going to kill me and came after me. He got a little busted up, but I had to do it." I shrugged it off. Her brother was a lightweight compared to the real badasses I'd taken on in the octagon.

"We will look at that footage. Ms. Sangare, I hope you get the rest you need. I'm sure Mr. Vandenberghe will make sure of it," the female officer gave Nina a smile.

"I sure will," I boasted as I placed a hand on Nina's belly.

"Thank you for your time, we'll let you rest now." With a wave all the officers were out the door.

I glanced down at Nina who was shaking her head,

she was clearly disappointed in how her parents handled the situation.

"Maybe we should just live our lives, you and me, without them," she suggested but I could instantly see in her eyes how much speaking those words broke her heart.

"I know you want your family to see Axel grow up and I know you don't mean those words," I told her. I knew her family meant so much to her, she wouldn't spend every Friday evening with them if they didn't matter but I could understand that she was hurt. "Give them time."

"I guess," she shrugged before my mom stepped up to us and placed a hand on my shoulder.

"I think my son is right," she noted as she agreed with me. "Time heals all wounds. Until then, you have our family and we love you as one of us, which is why I've been thinking about having a little something. It will be a joint wedding slash engagement party. We never had a celebration for Sophie and Basir's marriage and you two are engaged now. I want to do something in a couple weeks. Maybe you can invite your family."

"Maybe."

"It will be something to show them that you're taken care of and happy. Plus, our families can get to know one another." I tried my hardest to sound optimistic, but it was a long shot, her brother did try to kill me in a hospital waiting room after all.

CHAPTER SIXTEEN

NINA

My spirit was unsettled. My parents nor my brother were answering my calls and I was left as the outcast I'd expected to be. They'd disowned me for bringing shame to the family. I on the other hand, didn't understand the shame. I was happy for the first time in my life. I finally had the place I fit in and no longer felt completely alone in the world. I had Marc and our son.

I left the mosque near my home after making time to pray. I hoped that prayer would be the cure to my woes. Allah knew my heart and he made the path to my happiness. I prayed for my family to be able to see that this was all part of a purpose. Marc and I were a family.

Even with the stunt they pulled, calling the police on Marc, I was willing to put it behind us and forgive because having my son know my family was important to me. They had their flaws, but we all did. It was what made us human.

Arriving home as the rain started, I entered the building quickly and made my way to my apartment, grateful to be out of the drizzly, yet typical, Brussels weather. I unlocked the door to find Marc on the couch. We'd made the decision to stay in Brussels for the time being and put our search for a house in the countryside on hold. For now, I'd moved out of my apartment and into Marc's as he had more room and a spare bedroom for Axel.

"Come here, beautiful," Marc motioned with a crooked finger and patted his lap.

Strolling across the living room, I took my place on his lap and leaned in for a kiss. This was the comfortable life I was building, so different from my isolated life before.

"I don't think a hijab is supposed to be sexy, but I love when you wear it," Marc commented as he ran his thumb over my lips. "Something about your modesty is pretty fucking hot."

"Marc," I scolded him before allowing him to kiss me once more and deeper than before. "Mmm, je t'aime," I murmured against his lips before Axel decided he was being ignored for much too long and began to do backflips and pressing into my nerves. "Ouch."

"Hey little man, stop beating your maman up in here," Marc scolded my tummy.

"I thought of something crazy while at the mosque," I told Marc who sat up a little bit and gave me all his attention.

"What's that?" He asked as I began to take my headscarf off.

"We can just get married, like your sister and Basir. Just go to City Hall and do it. I don't want a big wedding anyway. I just want to be with you," I confessed. It was wild but now that Marc and I were no longer a secret, I wanted to jump in headfirst.

"Are you sure?" Marc asked with concern in his voice. I knew I wasn't acting like myself, but I'd changed so much in the last couple weeks. I was a different woman who was going to become a mother and I was ready to be a wife.

"More than sure. I want to be your wife. I've made the decision to say goodbye to my old life, and to the old me. I told you that day in New York I was becoming the girl I was always meant to be. Well, I think she's arrived." I shrugged and giggled at the sentiment.

"If you want, I want what you want," Marc easily declared. "When would you like to do it?"

"As soon as la maison de communale will allow us. Hell, tomorrow if we can."

I knew there was a possible wait. We couldn't just walk into city hall and get married. I knew in some communes you could wait up to six months to get your paperwork. I only prayed we wouldn't have to wait. I wanted to be his wife as soon as I legally could.

Marc gaped at me before the biggest grin spread across his face. I didn't want to wait or plan anything. I wanted to marry the man who pulled me from underwater. He was the man who saw my tears when I'd hid them from everyone for so long. He changed my world and I wasn't going to wait any longer to be his wife.

During prayer a thought came to me, I'd already been outcasted for the shame I brought to the family. I had two options, I could grovel and return to my old self, filled with depression or I could continue to live in the light and raise my son with Marc how it was intended. I'd made my decision easily. It was one I should have made for myself long ago.

"I'll need to let Fabumi know I need his best man services," Marc noted.

"And Ayo will be there one hundred percent. He's the only person in my family I've ever fully trusted and he's the only one talking to me." I used to be able to call my mom day or night and she'd answer my calls but now my calls go to voicemail. I left her a simple message each time, *"Bonjour Maman, c'est Nina. I just wanted to hear your voice, I love you and tell Papa I love him too. Have a lovely day. Bye."*

"Do you think you're ready for forever with the Belgian Beast?" Marc gave me a wink.

"I think I was ready for forever the day we met," I cooed as I wrapped my arms around his neck and ran the tips of my fingers over the back of his bald head. "You're my beast," I whispered before pressing my lips hard to his and absorbing the feel of him as his strong arms enveloped me.

———

MY NERVES WOULDN'T LET up. Inside I knew I was doing the right thing, but I couldn't help but have guilt for my family not being there to enjoy the day with me. I was lucky enough to have my cousin with me. We grew up the odd ones out in the family and supported each other always.

"Please tell me I'm not making a mistake," I begged Ayo as I stood in the restroom of city hall and stared back at my reflection.

I'd found a frosted blush pink lace fit and flare dress on discount. When I saw it, I knew. It was perfection and what I wanted to marry Marc in. We weren't traditional by any means from Belgian standard to my African Muslim heritage. We'd made our own rules and our wedding day was no different. We had only a few people in attendance and for me it was perfect.

When I first married, I had the big traditional Muslim wedding after the legal city hall ceremony. I gave my parents their dream once, I didn't want to repeat it again. I didn't want the spectacle. What I wanted was to share the moment of becoming husband and wife with the man I loved without the theatrics.

"You aren't making a mistake. You're taking control of *your* life because that's what it is, your life," Ayo asserted as he placed his hands on my shoulders and looked me directly in the eyes. "I know your struggle. You know I've lived the same one. We didn't want to rock the boat and be the odd ones out, but inevitably it happened. You've accepted that finally and you're the happiest I've ever seen you. I'm proud of you, big cousin."

"Thanks, little cousin," I beamed before he pulled me in for a tight hug.

I'd never been happier. For the first time, I didn't worry about what my family thought anymore at least I tried hard to not think about it. They'd made their decision when it came to me. I thought their love was unconditional, but I was clearly wrong. I knew with my son and any future children I would take a different path. I would encourage them to be who they wanted to be and love who they wanted without the fear of persecution under some archaic ideals.

Those ideals were what held me prisoner. I withheld myself from opportunities and allowed myself to drown in the storm of my depression. Today, there was no turning back. The scars on my wrist would always be a reminder of my past life but my new life was just beginning.

"This feels so different from last time," I commented as I picked up the bouquet Emmy had put together for me of delicate pink peonies. "I don't feel like I have this duty to anyone. It feels natural."

"That's because you're marrying a man you actually love. I might have to follow your lead," Ayo winked.

"Would this be with Tristan?" I questioned slyly of my cousin who'd been in a long-distance relationship with a guy he'd met in New York.

"Maybe, one day. Right now, it's too early to tell but

he's a good one," Ayo was just as happy as me for once. We were carving our own paths into the future.

I sighed as I thought of my parents. Charlotte and Luc were in attendance to support Marc, but my parents wouldn't even answer the calls of their only daughter. I had to face the fact our relationship might never be repaired but I also had to recognize I could never live up to their vision because for once I had my own.

"Hey, it will be all right," Ayo noted as we left the small restroom behind and stepped into the corridor where our few guests waited.

"I know. I just wish they could see it from my side, and I wish they could be here, but they are stuck in their ways. I can't change that." I shrugged it off.

"Stuck in the last century," Ayo joked.

"I invited them, though."

"Yeah, my parents called and asked if I was going. I told them hell yes, I was your maid of honor. Maman hung up on me," Ayo grinned at his insubordination, clearly proud of himself.

"You're ridiculous which is why I love you. Thanks for supporting me." I hugged my cousin once more before I got a glance at my groom who'd arrived with his best man at his side.

Marc had ditched his signature sweatpants for a pair of black slacks, which he wore with a black button up shirt, and a white tie. I'd only ever seen him so well dressed once, at my ballet performance, as he was usually very laid back no matter the circumstances. He was a fighter after all.

His eyes met mine from across the hall. He grinned proudly as he began in my direction with Fabumi rolling beside him and Emmy right behind holding their baby. As Marc approached, he wrapped an arm around my waist and pulled me to his side before leaning down and kissing my temple gently.

"Are you ready for this?" He whispered in my ear.

I peered up at him, his blue eyes boring back into mine. "More than ready," I told him truthfully. "I'm ready to be your wife."

"Good, because I can't fucking wait to be your husband."

"Nina Sangare and Marc Vandenberghe," our names were called from the other end of the hall.

Marc took my hand into his as we began toward the door where couples had gone in and out every few minutes for their civil ceremonies. We were greeted by a short, salt and pepper haired woman who gave us a kind smile.

"Bonjour, can I have your documents?" She asked as we entered the room where the ceremonies were performed. It was a small room that could fit twenty or so people and was decorated with fake plants and flowers.

Charlotte came from behind us and handed the woman the folders with our required documents. The woman flipped through the documents and confirmed our provided information and our signed declaration of marriage we'd managed to get the week prior. We were lucky as it was advised to book getting married six months in advance, but we managed in a couple of weeks to get a slot. I didn't know what magic was worked but I was going to go with it.

Marc squeezed my hand tightly. Looking up at him, the butterflies in my stomach danced along with baby Axel who I think could sense the excitement of the day.

"Je suis l'officier de l'état civil and I'll be performing your civil marriage ceremony," the woman introduced herself formally as she motioned for Marc and me to sit at the wooden table at the front of the small room.

Marc pulled out my chair where I sat before he took the seat next to mine. Under the table he laced our fingers and held onto me tightly.

We got to it rather quickly, l'officier de l'état civil read us our rights and the Belgian civil code as pertaining to marriage. In fifteen minutes, we'd heard the code, declared our dedication to one another, exchanged rings as we'd personally decided upon, and signed the registration book. Our witnesses Fabumi and Ayo signed their statement, paid the over three-hundred-Euro fee and were on our way.

Standing outside La Maison communale, Luc and Charlotte snapped photos of Marc and I holding the little leather-bound book which held our marriage certificate and kissing. I was a much different woman than the nervous wreck, twenty-one-year-old I was when I first married. There were a few photos left from the day in my parent's home, I didn't smile and if

I did it was more forced than anything. This time around, I couldn't stop beaming with the pure joy that flowed through me.

"How is this possible?" Marc asked as he stared at me in awe.

"I don't know but today is the best day," I easily declared as I stood on my toes and left a kiss on his lips.

"Okay lovebirds, let's go party!" Ayo cheered.

THE PARTY MARC'S mom had planned was now a joint marriage celebration for Marc and me, plus Sophie and Basir.

Charlotte had managed to book a restaurant not far from her home. Our friends, along with Marc and Basir's families filled the place to celebrate the two unions that had taken place. The only thing missing was having more of my family than just Ayo, but I would always be grateful for his support.

"You're a beautiful bride," Charlotte commented as she gave me her millionth hug of the day. "I'm so grateful Marc has you in his life. I don't think he'd ever admit it, but he'd fallen into this place of the usual day to day routine. The only thing he had was his fighting. He'd secluded himself when he wasn't fighting or at the gym. When he met you, he came out of the shell he'd buried himself in and for the first time I can see him living. You saved my son."

It was funny how people who are so different on the outside, like Marc and I, could be so incredibly similar on the inside. Trauma had taken its toll on both our lives and we were both forced into this whole of the usual, just living out our days with no real purpose outside our careers, but now we had each other.

"You'd be amazed at how much that was my life too," I commented with a smile to my groom who was across the room with a beer and chatting away with one of the guests.

Instantly my heart stopped as I spotted someone I knew well at the entrance of the room where our reception was taking place. My grandmother stood with Ayo behind her who was grinning from ear to ear. Charlotte turned to see what I was looking at and she gasped.

"Is that someone from your family?"

"My grandmother."

Standing from my seat, I made a beeline to my grandmother and cousin. Marc spotted me and stepped away from his conversation and joined me in reaching my grandma who gave me the biggest smile as she took my hands into hers.

"You look beautiful. Félicitations, mon trésor," she congratulated me as she held onto my hands tightly. I shook my head in disbelief. I never expected anyone to come around and the least expected was my incredibly tradition bound and religious grandmother.

"Mamy, what are you doing here?" I asked, still not believing she was standing right in front of me, plain as day with one of her favorite hijabs on which she only normally wore to celebrations.

Ayo laughed from behind her. "You hadn't noticed me leave, did you?"

I shook my head fiercely. "No."

"Mamy called me and said she wanted me to come pick her up. So, here she is," Ayo announced.

I had no words. I could only throw my arms around my grandmother and cry tears of joy I had that little bit more support than I'd ever expect.

"Oh, my little angel, I couldn't sit back and not support your happiness," she declared to me as she patted my arm. "Now, your old grandmother would like to have a seat."

"Of course," Marc suddenly went into gear and helped lead my grandmother to a table. I sat next to her as she held onto my hand and squeezed it tight, her graying eyes looking me over.

"Pregnancy is good on you," she commented in her soft voice. I inherited my low and sweet voice from her. "But happiness looks better. I could see the change in you over the months and I knew there was good in your life. We were all disappointed that day, but I think most of my disappointment was being left in the dark. I want to be a part of what brings my family joy."

"I'm sorry I kept it a secret for so long, but I was so afraid. You see the outcome. My parents hate me."

"They don't hate you, my dear. They will always love you with their whole hearts. They are disappointed but that night I told them that this life is too short to keep anger over things we can't control. I told them we should support you and love your child no matter how he or she was brought into this world. In Islam, children are always innocent no matter their conception. This baby," she placed her hand on my belly and gave a smile at feeling Axel's kicks. "Is innocent and loved deeply."

Tears dripped down my cheeks. Her support meant more to me than anything. I placed my hand over hers.

"Do you know what you're having?" She asked as Axel continued to kick away as he usually did. He was destined to be a handful.

"A baby boy," I told her as Marc came behind me and placed his hands on my shoulders.

"Al-ḥamdu lil-lāh," she sang her praises to Allah. "Un petit garçon."

"Axel Mohamed," I smiled as I told her the name we'd picked out for our son. "Would you like to meet my husband?"

"Of course." I don't think I'd ever seen my grandmother smile so much.

I easily motioned up to Marc who stood behind me with emotion in his eyes. He knew how much it'd hurt me to not have support from those I loved and now with even just my grandmother and Ayo, I had more than I could dream of.

"Enchanté, Madame," Marc bent to his knees to be at my grandma's eye level.

"Bonjour, young man. I hope you treat my granddaughter like the treasure she is. Do you hear me?" She was quick to assert herself over him.

I giggled as for the first time ever I saw Marc, the Belgian Beast, have the slightest bit of fear in his eyes as my short little grandmother grilled him.

"I have and will continue to treat your beautiful granddaughter with the utmost admiration," he declared.

"Good," she stated with a nod. "You seem like the type of man that will keep her protected and raise the child with a good example."

"Always, Madame."

"You know, I wasn't married when I became pregnant with my first child. My parents immediately made sure I married as quickly as possible to not allow my sin to bring shame upon the family. I was lucky that I loved that man dearly and he gave me two other children, but my parents never looked at me the same again. My prayer to Allah is that your parents find forgiveness in them, for you and your son. You are so much like me when I was young. I wasn't like everyone else and I locked myself away. My husband was the key to that lock, and I can see yours is for you." I'd never heard her story before. I never knew that she'd faced some of the same difficulties as me.

"There would be days when you were younger and would sleep all day and night. Your mother would just say you were being lazy, but I knew it was more because I saw myself. It's okay to be that way, sometimes we can't help it. I would try and talk to her about it, but she didn't want to listen. Maybe she'll learn to listen."

"Maybe," I said, feeling a little bit of hope flow through me. Maybe my parents would come around and accept the cards they were dealt. I was happy, that should be enough.

CHAPTER SEVENTEEN

MARC

My strength had returned with ferocity. Months of physical therapy had done my arm well and I would be back in the octagon and keeping my undefeated title. Until my first scheduled fight, I trained harder than I'd ever done. I wanted to be the force I was before plus more. I had so much to prove.

At only thirty years old, I had a few good years left in me I figured as average fighters retired from the sport in their mid-thirties. I'd made sure my name went down in the history books.

"Good use of that arm," Jean cheered as I spared with a fellow fighter. "Keep that speed too. You're looking good Marc."

In August, it was planned I'd be back in the U.S.A, this time in California. All eyes were on me as I strived to make my comeback.

Life had changed so much, and I took that with me as I fought. I'd defeated my most defeating voice. I no longer heard my father's voice putting me down and telling me I was worthless. I now heard my wife praising me and uplifting me as she did every day. We did that for each other.

Taking my partner to the ground, he tapped out and I declared victory. Standing up, Jean was applauding me, and Nina had arrived standing next to him with a smile on her face and a hand on her belly that was ready to blow. With only two months until her due date, we were knee deep into planning for our son's arrival.

I lent a hand to my practice partner and helped him to his feet before we both left our gym's octagon and I jogged immediately down to Nina and pulled her into my arms.

"Marc, you're covered in sweat," she complained as she tried to shove my sweaty body off her.

"You don't say that in bed when I'm working my magic," I grumbled seductively into her ear.

"It's not the same," she argued playfully as she shoved me once more and I reluctantly let her go. I looked her over. It was one of the few times she wore more traditional African clothing. Her dress was colorful and filled with intricate patterns and the scarf on her head covering her hair completely, matched.

She had this light about her as she beamed at me. She wasn't the same woman I'd met back at the train station in September. That woman was timid and scared. She only had one thing keeping her from drowning. Now she carried this confident spirit that was infectious. Every night, I couldn't wait to get home and be wrapped in her aura.

I was anxious for what the future held for us. Our son would arrive soon, and Nina was still at odds with her family but there was hope that would change as it was the final night of Ramadan and her grandmother had invited us over to feast with the family after nightfall.

"I'm going to shower and then I'll be ready to go," I told her with a kiss on her cheek before I started toward the locker room.

My knowledge of the Islamic faith was limited to what I did know from friends and Basir, but I'd learned so much more being with Nina. She wasn't overzealous in her beliefs, but she did hold them dear to her. She'd grown up with faith being a large part of her life. I on the other hand had grown up as a number of Belgians with a more agnostic view on faith. My parents had both been raised Catholic but weren't particularly strict on bringing my sister and I up with any faith-based cornerstone.

Nina and I stayed up late often talking about how we'd raise our son. We'd come from two different places when it came to faith and we'd have to merge those into one. It was going to be an interesting challenge, but we were both up to it. At the end of the day we both agreed what was most important was he was healthy and happy.

Finishing my shower, I dressed a bit nicer than I normally did. My usual sweatpants, aka the key to seducing Nina, would have to take a backseat for me to formally meet her family. I buttoned up my shirt and pulled on my dark jeans which I figured kept it a little casual and not overly formal. I'd never been to a Ramadan celebration and didn't know what to expect.

Nina chatted with Jean while she awaited my arrival. Her hands as usual were placed on her belly and I'm sure Axel was murdering her insides with his strong kicks. That boy was meant to be an MMA fighter.

"Looking good there, son," Jean mentioned as I approached.

"I hope it's okay," I noted to Nina who gave me a warm smile.

"It's perfect," she cooed as she tried to stand but was failing the battle with her round belly in front of her.

I presented her with my hands and pulled her to her feet.

"I don't know how I'm to survive another two months like this."

"You'll do it," I reassured as I laced our fingers.

We said our goodbyes to Jean and left the gym behind. Walking slow as Nina waddled along, we arrived at the parking garage where in a reserved spot our car awaited. Becoming a father meant making some changes and parking my motorbike to get a car.

I helped Nina into our new BMW SUV before I hopped in myself and we were off toward Nina's parent's home, where the family's celebration was taking place.

Cruising down the ring, I glanced in Nina's direction. She was chewing her bottom lip and her fingers toyed with the fabric of her dress. Reaching over I gripped her hand tightly to reassure her. Two months had passed since she'd last seen or had any real contact with her parents besides the daily voicemail she left her mom in hopes she came around and answered the phone one day.

"I can sense things won't go well," she murmured as she peered out the window and I took the exit into Halle.

"Where is my optimistic petite danseuse?" I rubbed her hand in hopes of encouraging her.

"She's worried but Mamy said she wouldn't let anything happen and she'd keep the peace," Nina noted as we began down the small residential street where her parents lived. She gripped onto my hand. "I have to keep the faith. It has been thirty days of fasting, prayer, and reflection. I hope everyone used their time wisely."

I'd never known what the holiday was for until Nina explained the month was more than just fasting until nightfall but prayer, reflection, and community. Nina didn't take part in the fasting due to her pregnancy, but she dedicated herself to prayer, volunteered a bit at the mosque near our apartment, and I'd catch her up late at night writing in her journal as she liked to do to reflect.

"Here goes nothing," Nina commented with a nervous sigh.

I parked the car and quickly got out and jogged

around to help Nina out. With her hand secured in mine, we began the short walk from where we parked to her parent's front door.

Nina rang the bell and moments later the door opened to her mother who sneered instantly at the sight of us.

"What are you doing here?" she snapped ferociously.

"Mamy invited us," Nina said, her voice small.

"Est-ce Nina?" Her grandmother's voice called from inside the house.

Her mother only grumbled something under her breath before allowing us in the house.

"Maybe we should just go," Nina whispered to me.

"Your grandmother invited us. We can stay for a little bit. I think it will be good," I tried to sound optimistic, but things were already going downhill fast.

I followed Nina into the modest home she shared with her parents when they left Brussels until she was married to her first husband. I spotted a photo I recognized that Nina had in her old bedroom of herself as a teenager with braces.

We entered the living room filled with people who all seemed to go silent with our entrance. I placed my arm protectively around Nina's waist as I spotted her brother sitting on the couch with a very pregnant woman. He glared at me as if he was stabbing me with a thousand knives.

"Eid Mubarak tout le monde," Nina said in a shaky voice.

"Eid Mubarak, ma petite," Nina's grandmother said with a grand smile as she motioned for us to come to her. A path was made as we stepped in her grandma's direction. We each took turns leaning down and giving her a kiss on the cheek. "So much bigger than when I last saw you." She rubbed Nina's large belly.

A woman and Nina's mom began to chat in a language I didn't know nor understand as Ayo stood and greeted us as well before he gave his seat to Nina.

"What are they speaking?" I asked Nina as I leaned over to her.

"Bambara. It's one of the main languages of Mali," Nina answered me. "I only know a few words. I never learned to speak it."

"And who is the woman your mom is talking to?" I asked intrigued by who everyone was and what was going on around me.

"My aunt. My dad's sister."

"My mom," Ayo interjected from next to me.

I'd been in some awkward situations but this one took the cake. Nina was an outcast in her own family. She'd never fit in, but they always accepted her. Now no one spoke to her, even her own mother who continued to glare as she chatted in a language Nina didn't fully understand. Maybe Nina was right. Perhaps we shouldn't have come.

"Nina," a voice from the other end of the couch spoke up. "When are you due?" I peered to see a woman who also had a huge rounded stomach and two children climbing on her lap. This had to be Nina's sister-in-law whom I'd been warned about.

"July thirteenth," Nina told her politely.

"Only about two weeks *after* me," the woman announced proudly as if she had a leg up on Nina for being due first.

Noise came from the hallway and the man I knew was Nina's father strolled into the living room with a large platter in his hand and a huge smile until his eyes landed on Nina and his smile faded.

"What is she doing here?" He shot angrily with a nod directly in Nina's direction. "And with that man?"

"Your mother invited them," Nina's mother was quick to point out.

"That I did. This is a time for family and Nina as well as her wonderful husband are family," her grandmother asserted for everyone to hear.

"Maybe Marc and I should go," Nina surrendered as she glanced up at me, I squeezed her shoulder ready to do whatever she wanted.

"Nonsense," her grandmother shot. "I won't see my granddaughter run out of here simply because she pursued her happiness. Maybe she didn't go about it the traditional way, but she found the one person who gives her joy and they are going to have a child. Her child is innocent, and he deserves to be welcomed into this family as every other child. I don't want any more of this nonsense. We will enjoy this meal together as a family. Do you hear me?"

"Oui, maman," Nina's father reluctantly answered before he turned out the room.

"The goat has arrived, and we'll eat soon," her grandmother told me happily. "First, the Iftar."

"What's that?" I asked genuinely wanting to know everything.

"We will eat dates to respect Muhammad's practice of breaking the fast with three dates. We will then pray and eat," Nina explained to me expertly. I loved learning from her. It was part of our dynamic, learning from one another.

It wasn't long before Nina's father returned with a platter stacked with dates. He handed them out to everyone and came to us. He shook his head as he looked Nina over with her large pregnant belly.

After eating the dates, the family dispersed to find places to pray. Nina and I stayed put in the living room. Nina said her prayers while I watched. Her dedication to her faith was mesmerizing. I only went to church a few times a year and to watch someone like Nina who took her faith seriously was dazzling in a new way.

Minutes later, the family shuffled into an outdoor veranda area where a long table was set up for the feast. Nina and I took a seat with her grandmother and Ayo. Sitting directly across from me was Jaheem, Nina's brother. Before tonight, I hadn't seen him since the hospital.

As the food was served, one of Nina's cousins struck up a conversation with her. I could see why Nina wanted to have her family around, they were lively and when all together they filled the room with joy. Axel deserved to enjoy the diversity of our two families combined.

"How can you all sit here like this is normal?" Jaheem suddenly outburst. "You're breaking bread with the man who took advantage of Nina."

"Jaheem, please," Nina's grandmother begged.

"Please nothing. She brings this sale blanc into our family home on this holy day," Jaheem stood from his chair to make his point and I stood as well. I wouldn't put up with his nasty words. "You've tainted my sister and now you sit with my family."

"You don't want to continue down this path," I warned him sternly a deep growl erupting from my throat.

"Marc, love," Nina's quiet voice came as she placed a hand on my arm in hopes of calming me down, but I was already heated.

"You've tricked my sister, you've raped her, you've defiled her," Jaheem continued his taunting.

"Just a weak pussy," my father's voice added into the fray. I'd gone so long without it's taunting and now it was triggered back into my mind.

"Shut up," I growled.

"Rapist," he spat.

"You're not a man. You can never be a man," my father slurred as he did when he yelled his insults in my direction.

The only thing I saw before my eyes was the color red as I leapt over the table in one swift motion. I took

Jaheem to the floor. My fists laying into him with everything. It wasn't just Jaheem I was fighting but my father. The years of his words, beating, and abuse all seemed to come to a head, and I couldn't stop. I could barely hear the screams around me as I fought people off me until I heard the scream of Nina's name.

"Someone call 112," I heard a woman scream.

"Nina, Nina, are you okay?" I heard her mother's voice question.

I stopped instantly and jumped off her brother before I turned in the direction of the voices. Nina was against the wall, sitting on the floor, her hands holding her belly as she cried out in agony.

"Nina!" I jumped in her direction but was stopped easily by her mother's hand pressing to my chest and keeping me from reaching my wife.

"Don't you dare," she snapped. "This is because of you. Don't you dare go near my daughter. I won't have you hurt her again."

"Hurt her?" I questioned easily confused to what I'd done. I'd never touched her. I would never hurt Nina intentionally, ever.

With a hand on my shoulder, I turned to see Ayo who only gave me a nod. I didn't understand. What had happened? I glanced to Nina who was still crying out and gasping at the pain she was experiencing.

"She tried to get you off Jaheem," Ayo told me. I shook my head not remembering Nina coming to me at all. "You practically tossed her across the room, and she hit the wall."

"No," I gasped unable to believe I'd physically hurt my wife. Not my wife. I'd never hurt her. I loved her too much to even think about anything so terrible. "Nina, ma petite danseuse." I couldn't even try to step in her direction as she was surrounded by the women who tried to keep her calm.

In the distance, I already heard the sounds of the ambulance coming. My heart pounded intensely as I thought of not just Nina but our son. I'd never hurt them, never, but knowing I had was hard to think about. I quickly wiped away the tears that began to prickle the corner of my eyes.

It wasn't long before we were joined with paramedics, and policemen. I recognized the two policemen from the hospital before. They spoke to Nina's family as both Nina and her brother were placed onto gurneys. The policemen approached me with handcuffs, and I understood why. I wanted to go to the hospital with Nina, but I knew that wouldn't be happening.

"I'm sorry, ma petite danseuse," I said to her as she was rolled past me. "I'm so sorry." I sobbed watching her leave the room knowing I might never be welcomed into her life again. I could have very well lost her, forever.

CHAPTER EIGHTEEN

NINA

My heart refused to stop thumping wildly even after the doctors pumping in multiple medications into me to calm me down. I couldn't be calm when I'd witnessed and experienced the man I loved become the monster I feared inside of him.

Sitting next to me, my mother gripped my hand as I laid in the labor and delivery unit. The force of Marc knocking me into the wall with my emotional distress had caused me to go into preterm labor. At that moment, my contractions were gone as the doctors gave me medications by injection to stop them.

"I don't see any more contractions on the screen," my mother mentioned as she stared at one of the machines I was hooked to.

"No, I'm not feeling any," I told her as I placed my hand on my belly. Axel kicked at my hand and I smiled knowing that my little boy was perfectly okay.

My night was dramatic with doctors rushing

around in hopes of stopping my labor and calming me down. I was hysterical and inside I could still feel it with my rapidly beating heart.

"Nina, ma petite, I'm so sorry with how everything has happened. I wish I could take this all back. I should have supported you. I really should have," my mom cried with tears flowing down her cheeks.

"Maman," I sighed as I squeezed her hand. "Don't apologize. I understand. I only wished I never had to keep secrets and I could have been open from the beginning. I'm now just a little lost on what I should do. Marc has been good to me, but he has this part inside him that I've only seen come out once before and that part scares me."

"You are always welcome home. You and the baby can live with me and your father. I'm here to support you from now on. I can't nearly lose my daughter again." I saw it in my mother's eyes. She meant every word. She was ready to put it behind us, but I wasn't sure about my father. He would tolerate me around, but he would still be difficult.

"I need to talk to Marc. He's not that violent man. I know he's not," I insisted. I knew he wasn't that monster. He wasn't really his persona. They may have called him the Belgian Beast, but Marc wasn't a beast, he was my husband who'd gone through trauma. It was time he no longer fought it away but truly worked through it.

"He was at the police station, but Ayo says his trainer picked him up this morning," my mom told me.

I nodded. Knowing Marc would've wanted to come directly to the hospital but I'm sure he was cautious and didn't come because my family would be around. "If you'll be happy, I am willing to accept him into our lives. He's clearly made you happy and loves you, but I worry."

"I do too. But that man you saw last night, that's not Marc. Marc is kind, he's gentle, and loving. He has a temper when provoked. Jaheem was also in the wrong for what he said to Marc. He should have never called him those things, especially a rapist. Marc never forced me into anything. My love for him has always been consensual." I had to make sure she wouldn't take sides in the matter. I loved my brother, but Jaheem deserved what he got. You don't poke a bear and expect to not be mauled.

"Jaheem was completely wrong. He ruined our night." My mom shook her head. "I'm so disappointed. Before it though, you and Marc seemed to be having a good time. He was so attentive to you."

"Always," I gushed as I thought of my husband who never let a moment pass without him paying complete attention to my needs.

"What shocked me the most was how willing this white man was to know our customs and our faith. I would have never expected that ever, especially in the past few years with the attacks and all. Around Belgium and the world everyone in the Muslim faith has been put under this microscope. We've been branded as terrorists and outsiders, not part of the larger community. It's already hard enough for us being black, but here is this white man in our family home who is willing to learn from you in order to love you."

I grinned at how my mother realized our differences could bring us together. Marc cared enough about me to accept every part of me, even my persecuted religion. We were all alike. We all lived our lives, no matter who we were or where we came from. Straight or Gay, Muslim, Christian, Jewish, or Atheist, man or woman, black or white, brown or yellow. We all lived out these incredibly beautiful and electrified lives that none of us should be persecuted for. We all loved the same. I loved Marc no matter our circumstances and dramatic differences.

"He's good for you and I think you're good for him," she noted.

"He is. My life will never be the same. I'm a different woman now," I easily declared because I was different. My story began with me living in this cycle of depression. Now I felt like the chains had been broken.

"I do have something else to apologize for. Your father and I should have never filed that complaint saying Marc had taken advantage of you. We were in the wrong for that one. I hate I played a part in hurting my own child. I don't know if I can forgive myself for that one." I knew my mom meant what she said. I still had a hard time accepting they'd done it, but they had. I reflected on it a lot during Ramadan and I was willing to accept her apology as we were in a season of healing. "It was disgusting of us."

"It was. I agree with that. I think that hurt the most. You could have disowned me and been done with me but instead you chose to hurt me and the man I love. I am willing to put it behind us. I really am if we can all work together to create a happy and loving environment for my son." That was my only condition. Axel would enter the world to two families that loved him and were willing to work together for him.

"I can completely agree to that, ma petite. I won't say that means I accept Marc without fault right now. He did land both my children in the hospital. I'm cautious, but I won't intervene in your relationship. Your son does need his father but I'm wary." My mother expressed her concerns.

"Understandable. Very understandable. I told you though, Marc isn't that man. He's the attentive man you saw who loves me and our son," I explained to her.

"I need to see more of that but right now I can't completely let him in."

I nodded in response as I understood, and I knew I couldn't force it. The relationship had to grow naturally. "Je t'aime," she said rubbing my arm.

"Je t'aime, maman."

———

UNLOCKING the door to the apartment I shared with Marc, I didn't know what to expect. I'd spoken to Marc over text message but that was it. He was remorseful for the situation and had even sought professional help for his anger issues. He had to face his day in court for the assault on my brother and we awaited the outcome of it.

Marc stood up as I entered the living room after my parents dropped me off at home. I was under doctor's orders to take it easy after spending a week in the hospital.

I saw the sorry in his eyes as I approached him. He took my hands into his as we sat together on the couch. I didn't know where to start with him.

"How are you feeling today?" He anxiously asked as he stroked the back of my hand with his thumb.

"Better. I'm glad to be out of the hospital. I think Axel is ready to have some slightly better food," I joked lightly, pulling a smile from Marc.

"I missed you and your spirit around here," he told me as he swept one of my braids behind my ear. "I saw my therapist this morning. It was a good session. We're going to work on ways I can de-escalate my anger before it gets the best of me."

"I'm proud of you," I said truthfully. It wasn't something men were the most willing to do. Therapy was a big step and I appreciated the fact that Marc, this big muscular man, was willing to admit his flaws and seek the help available.

My fingers traced the tattoos on his arms as we sat together in the home we'd been working to get ready to bring a baby to.

"I'm still hurt though. You broke your promise. You'd promised I'd never have to see that monster again and I did. This time I was collateral damage. That hurt like hell not just physically but mentally. I felt like I'd made this grave mistake, being with you and I hated that feeling because I know it wasn't a mistake. We aren't a mistake," I concluded with him.

Marc nodded in agreeance.

"We aren't but I made one. Yes, I broke my explicit promise to you. I never wanted to be that monster around you, and I promise I won't. This time my promise is real and binding. My fight next month will be my last. I'm going to retire. Jean has offered me a job training fighters in the gym. I want to be here and present with you and Axel. I think giving up the fight will help keep the monster under wraps and maybe get rid of him for good."

I was in shock Marc would ever give up his career but at the same time I knew it was time. He'd eclipsed any expectations and would go down in the history books. He'd forever be the Belgian Beast and now it was time to pass that legacy on.

"Thank you," I whispered as I leaned toward him and kissed him gently. It was time to fight for our love and fight for our family.

"Anything for you and this little guy." He rubbed my stomach. "And future little guys and girls."

"I like the sound of that. Our own little tribe," I smiled as I leaned into his arms and allowed him to envelope me with his strength.

"I'm going to raise my children as a man should. I'm going to love the hell out of them, and they are never going to have empty stomachs and never fear the monster. My father helped grow the monster in me and it is time to let him go the same way I let the man go." Marc had his work cut out for him, but I was in it with him. We were a family until the end.

"Just promise me one thing," I said as I peered up at him.

"Anything."

"Just be here and keep being the man I fell in love with. The compassionate man who saw me suffering and pulled me out of that. I'm here to do the same for you whenever you need it."

"Always, ma petite danseuse, always."

EPILOGUE

MARC

Watching her on stage never got old. The way her body gracefully moved across the stage was the most mesmerizing thing I'd ever witnessed. Nina was captivating and there was no doubt she was where she belonged when performing and as prima ballerina.

After three children, she was still a wonder and her return to the opera house had been anticipated by dance aficionados worldwide. The show was sold out. It reminded me of some of my best fights when there wasn't an empty seat in the house and as she and the other ballerinas took their bows, we all stood and applauded loudly. I tossed a bouquet of pink peonies on stage, the same flowers she carried the day we married.

Leaving the building, I stalked around the side as I used to do when Nina and I first met, and I'd pick her up after performances. My heart would beat faster and faster every time the side door opened until she emerged with her bag over her shoulder, looking like the beautiful woman she'd always been to me.

"Let me get that for you," I took her bag from her shoulder and threw it over my own. I bent to her lips and gave her a gentle kiss. Our kisses still reminded me of our first months together. They were just as fresh and just as new even in our chaotic world. "You did great tonight."

"Thanks, love," she leaned into my arms as we began to walk together toward the garage I'd parked our car in. "I feel like I could have done better but I always say that. How are the kids?"

"Your mom texted me," I told her as I pulled my phone from my pocket. "The kids are fast asleep. Natasha was a little fussy, but your mom eventually got her to sleep, too."

Axel was about three months old when Nina's mother finally accepted me. She could see the man I really was. I wasn't a monster and I loved the hell out of her daughter and grandson. The catalyst was Nina had returned to the stage and I was alone with Axel who screamed for his mother constantly. I didn't know what to do but with Nina's parents living near as we'd only just moved, I caved and called her mother for help.

Lola Sangare had some secrets up her sleeve. I'd started calling her "The Baby Whisperer" that night. She taught me so much and I was grateful I could be a better father because of her. We formed a unique bond that night and she saw I only wanted what was best for my family.

I showed her the photo her mom had sent of our oldest two, my boys, Axel and Hakim, passed out in bed together followed by another photo of our eight-month-old baby girl in her bassinet. Our baby girl was named after Nina's grandmother who'd passed away just before her birth.

It was funny, the relationship that formed between me and the rest of Nina's family after everything. They finally saw us for what we were, happy. I attended every family event with Nina and the kids, and Jaheem and I even got along after I'd spent a couple weeks in jail over the assault. He and I would watch football together and feud over our chosen favorite teams. It took until Axel was nearly a year old before Nina's father fully came around. He'd been trying to find a new way to exercise to prevent another heart attack. He'd been a fan of boxing and I offered to coach him a couple times a week to keep him active. He accepted and we bonded as well.

"I'm starving," Nina commented as we reached the car and I was struck with an idea. It was one of those few nights we didn't have the kids and maybe a little impromptu date would be perfect for us hard working parents.

"Let's put your things in the car and go grab a little something to eat before going home," I unlocked the car and placed her bag in the trunk before closing it and taking her hand into mine. "You deserve it. You're the hardest working woman I know."

Every single day I tried my hardest to spoil the fuck out of my wife. She'd given me everything I'd missed and needed in my life. She deserved every single moment for her I could provide because she saved me from my demons, but if you heard it from her, she'd say I saved her.

"I think I know where we're going," Nina jested as she jabbed her elbow into my side. I grabbed my abs in mock pain as she giggled away. Her laughter still got me right in the heart. So innocent and sensual at the same time.

"Figured a little blast from the past would be nice," I commented with my arm back around her waist as we strolled toward The Grand Place.

I could never forget our first date. Taking my ballerina out for dinner and sharing our first kiss in the market square.

We chatted lightly on our walk. In the more recent days, we never got much time to just talk like we used to about anything and everything when we had two wild little boys running around and a new baby girl demanding attention.

We arrived at the little Greek restaurant we'd had our first date at. I opened the door and motioned for Nina to step inside first before I followed her in.

"Bonsoir," we were greeted right away.

"Bonsoir, une table pour deux s'il vous plait," I requested as I settled my hand on Nina's lower back.

She leaned into my body and glanced up at me, her brown eyes shitting through her long eyelashes.

"This way," the waiter directed us to a small table for two and if I remembered right, it was the same table from the very night I got to kiss Nina for the first time.

Taking our seats, I took Nina's hands into mine and held them tightly. My stunning wife and my entire my life sat across from me. I was amazed every day that I still held the love of the dark-skinned beauty I'd met in Central Station.

"Ma petite danseuse," I cooed as I toyed around with her wedding ring.

"My Belgian Beast," she purred in return. "Look at us. Some days I can't believe it and then I look at our three beautiful children and I believe every moment from the joyous ones to the bad ones. It's all us and perfect in a way."

"Our imperfection makes us perfect I think," I noted as we weren't perfect, but we'd carved our own little piece of perfection.

NINA

After dinner, we didn't hang around too long. We got directly in the car and started on the drive home. After Axel was born, we began our search for a home in the country. I wanted to be closer to my parents and

Fabumi already lived in an idyllic town only fifteen minutes from them. We found the perfect home in Enghien for our family that was just beginning to grow as not long after we moved, I discovered I was pregnant with our second son.

I loved the life we were able to build. Marc had his final fight and that was it. He retired as promised. He took up coaching instead and I could tell that in the end it made him happier than fighting ever could. Jean retired a year ago and left the gym to Marc to be the lead coach while the practical business part was left to Fabumi. The best friends worked great together, and my husband came home every day with a smile on his face.

The best part was the relationship I eventually formed with my parents. It was nothing like we'd ever had. We were actually close and I was able to be candid with them in a way my brother had always been but not myself. My mom and I spoke at length about my depression and she was able to see my side and know I wasn't being lazy or antisocial but mentally I was hurting. She'd become my best friend and I could relate to her as a mother.

I was constantly amazed that I'd carried three lives inside me. Three perfect little lives. Our two sons and one daughter were our entire world. When I saw them, I saw the fight Marc and I put up to escape our past demons and give life to a new generation that wouldn't be hindered by those voices.

"Dinner was amazing," I commented as Marc pulled into the driveway of our modest brick home.

Marc's hand slid over my lap and gripped at my inner thigh. I moaned at his dominant touch. Though Marc no longer fought, he was still the Belgian Beast in our bedroom. I was grateful for this rare night where our children were sleeping at my parent's and we had the house to ourselves.

"Come on, let's get inside," Marc instructed me. He didn't have to tell me twice. I leaped from my seat and out of the car.

Marc met me at the front door and opened it. Stepping inside, I didn't have the time to think as Marc slammed the door and pressed my body against the wall. Hiking my leg up, he reached under my dress and yanked my panties down my legs.

"Bedroom," I murmured as his lips left fiery kisses on my neck and down over my collarbone.

"I need you now," he growled against my heated skin. Now it was he who pulled his hard dick from his pants, lifted my legs around his waist and thrusted into me.

I gasped into the air as Marc rammed into me, my body pressed to the wall. He was the ultimate lover in my eyes. He'd been since our first time together, and now he was my husband who cared for me in every single way. He was the father of my children and kept us not wanting for anything.

"Marc," I cried out as my hands gripped tightly as him.

"Not yet, ma petite danseuse," he growled as he pulled me away from the wall and began carrying me through house. Navigating through halls and over discarded toys, we arrived in our bedroom where he dropped me to the bed.

I watched as Marc dropped his pants and kicked them off. He fought each of the buttons on his button up shirt before ripping it from his arms. He stood over me, the streetlights reflecting off his rock-hard body.

"Take your dress off," he commanded, and I was quick to pull the dress over my head. Leaning down over me, Marc reached behind me and unhooked my bra, leaving me completely bare as he laid me back on the bed. "Perfect," he murmured before he bent and sucked one of my nipples into my mouth.

As he sucked at my flesh, he spread my legs and his fingers dipped into my awaiting wetness and grazed over my sensitive bud. I moaned and slid my hands over his bald head as his stroking fingers matched that of his tongue.

Pulling up, Marc flipped me to my side and slipped behind me. He easily lifted my nimble leg and pushed inside me from behind. His arm wrapped around me and gripped my body tightly as he rode into me.

"Touch yourself," he grumbled before my hands slipped down my bare body and between my legs to my clit.

Doing as I was told; I rubbed my fingers over my engorged bud until my cries filled the room along with Marc's growls before he spilled into me.

Coming down from our highs, I faced him, and he pulled me to his chest. In the dim light, I could just make out his latest tattoo, our daughter's name. My fingers traced the letters of her name on his chest and I grinned up at him.

"I remember the day I told you I was afraid you'd disappear and years later, you're still here, loving me just as you promised," I reminded him of that night in his apartment. One of our first times together when we were so new to one another. "Sometimes I'm amazed."

"Me too," he chuckled.

"Why?" I asked him curious.

"I'm amazed that this beauty still loves this beast."

"Stay fucking used to it," I joked as I played with Marc's own words.

He took my face into his hands and kissed me with all his might. The love of my life, my husband, and the father of my children. My Belgian Beast.

Nothing is chance, there's always a purpose.

THE END

ACKNOWLEDGMENTS

This book was a labor of love from the first word. There is a reason I dedicated this book to the beautiful country of Belgium. I've lived in Belgium since 2011. I gave birth in this country and I work in this country. I've experienced the horror of terror attacks in this country, but I've also embraced the multiculturality that makes up this country especially the capital city of Brussels.

This book is a love story in and to Belgium through the eyes of my most diverse characters yet. Yes, I write interracial romance and my cast of characters is always diverse but there was something different about this book. First, this is the first book where none of my main characters are American. I wanted to write a story homegrown in Belgium but also be an immigrant story. Belgium is full of immigrant culture and it had to be a staple of this book.

Next, I wanted to take away the mask of the usual romance book characters. It is I think even if not mentioned that the characters in romance novels even if not white are by and large assumed to default as Christian. We forget that the biggest religion on earth is Islam and there are more followers of Islam in this world than Christianity. A good majority of immigrants are Muslim, especially in Belgium. I wanted to turn the tables and show that romance is for everyone no matter their religion, sexual orientation, or color. Marc and Nina were a love story that needed to be told through a different lens than the usual.

I want to take the time to thank a few people. To a woman who I've been able to message constantly with my questions about Islam and Muslim families, I want to thank the lovely author Sara Allen for all her help. My understanding of Islam I think is usual for most people who don't practice the religion and I needed to dig in much deeper than a Google search, Sara offered her assistance and was my biggest help in telling Nina's story.

Thank you to my Belgians, beginning with my husband, Olivier, for my language assistance, and friends Lauren and Ann. Also a huge thank you to my expat friends living here as well, Genevieve and Keila.

I truly hope everyone has enjoyed this story. I stepped outside my box and it delivered a beautiful love story that I am definitely proud of.

Thanks to Out of Your Write Mind for the beta reading services along with my other Beta Readers

Simone Choi and Amanda McCoy. As always, thank you to Nicole Davis for her editing services, and to Julie Lafrance for proofing.

All my love,

Janae

ABOUT THE AUTHOR

Janae Keyes is an American mom, wife, and hopeless romantic living in Europe. She loves to explore various cultures coming together through the magic of love. Residing in a suburb of Brussels, Belgium, with her husband and daughter, Janae loves to share her passion for romance with others.

For more from Janae visit:
www.JanaeKeyes.com

- facebook.com/JanaeKeyesAuthor
- twitter.com/JanaeKeyesWrite
- instagram.com/JanaeKeyesAuthor
- amazon.com/author/janaekeyes
- bookbub.com/profile/janae-keyes

ALSO BY JANAE KEYES

Broken Politics

Sleepless Fate

The Champagne Bubbles Series

Hearts On Ice

Past Transgressions: A Russian Roulette Love Story

Homegoing

Never the Bride

Would Smell As Sweet

A Misconception of Loyalty

Influenced: A Good Girl, Bad Boy Love Story

Lady Guardians: Born to Ride

Pleasing the Professor

Decadence & Danger

All can be found on Amazon

Made in the USA
Monee, IL
02 December 2021